"I don't understand why you're not married, Melissa,"

David said bluntly. "I mean, you love children, that's obvious, and from the way the fellows at the fund-raiser were looking at you, I'd say you could attract about any man you wanted."

"I guess that's your answer." She lightly tossed her head. "I haven't found one that I wanted."

"That picky, huh?" His grin teased her.

"Very," she agreed. She disagreed with people who said you should compromise with life. Her faith wouldn't let her willingly make a bad decision and throw the future away.

"What about you? There are plenty of eligible women who would be very happy to be Mrs. David Ardell."

"But you're not one of them," he said lightly, as if teasing her.

Books by Leona Karr

Love Inspired

Rocky Mountain Miracle #131
Hero in Disguise #171

LEONA KARR

A native of Colorado, the author has always been inspired by God's magnificence and the delights in using mountain valleys, craggy cliffs and high, snow-tipped peaks as a setting for many of her books. She began writing professionally in 1980 and has enjoyed seeing more than thirty of her romance books in print. The theme of "love conquers all" is an important message in all her stories.

Even though Leona contracted polio the year before the vaccine was approved, the blessings in her life have been many. "Wheeling and dealing" from a wheelchair, she has helped raise four children, pursued a career as a Reading Specialist and recently, after being widowed for five years, found a new love and soul mate in her own "Love Inspired" marriage.

She strives to write stories that will enrich the spiritual lives of those who read them, and is grateful to the many readers who have found her books filled with warm, endearing characters that they can identify with.

Hero in Disguise

Leona Karr

Love Inspired®

Published by Steeple Hill Books™

STEEPLE HILL BOOKS

Steeple
Hill™

ISBN 0-373-87178-3

HERO IN DISGUISE

Copyright © 2002 by Leona Karr

Visit us at www.steeplehill.com

Printed in U.S.A.

Call unto me and I will answer you,
and will tell you great and hidden things
which you have not known.

—*Jeremiah* 33:3

With thanks to Paul Fanshane,
a very special and delightful friend

Chapter One

Let me say and do the right thing, Melissa Chanley prayed as she entered the Colorado State Capital.

It wasn't going to be easy, no matter how she approached David Ardell. The contents of the folded note in her purse were going to shake up the handsome young attorney's life the minute he laid his eyes on it.

How would he react? She'd never met him personally, but she'd seen his picture in the newspaper with the governor, and on television. He was in his early thirties, had wavy hair almost the color of old gold and dark brown eyes. In public he was poised, articulate and successful—but what kind of person lay under that successful political veneer? Was there a compassionate nature that she could appeal to?

As she opened the door to the outer office, Melissa hoped she wasn't embarking on a fool's errand. A middle-aged secretary with graying hair sat behind a computer. A wooden desk placard identified her as

Elsie Shaw. She gave Melissa a practiced smile and
an enquiring raise of her eyebrows. Curiosity was evident as her frank gaze assessed Melissa.

"May I help you?"

"I'm Melissa Chanley. I have a two o'clock appointment."

When Melissa made the appointment, the secretary
had enquired as to the reason for the meeting, but
Melissa had sidestepped the question. In her capacity
as freelance writer for Colorado's *Women of the West*
magazine, Melissa had learned to save explanations
for the person she was interviewing, and even though
her appointment had nothing to do with her professional occupation, she wasn't about to share that with
his secretary.

"Oh, yes, Ms. Chanley. I'll let him know you're
here." She spoke briskly into the intercom, listened
a moment and then nodded. Turning to Melissa, she
said, "He'll see you now, but only for a few minutes.
Mr. Ardell has a busy schedule this afternoon." She
left her desk, opened an adjoining office door, motioned Melissa inside and then quietly closed the door
behind her.

Melissa hesitated just inside the office as her
sweeping gaze quickly assessed the room, which was
crowded with more furniture than any decent interior
decorator would allow. Large windows were banked
by bookcases and a collection of scenic western oil
paintings was mounted on the opposite wall. A ring
of chairs took up space in the center of the room as
if left by a previous meeting, and a large executive

desk was loaded with books and papers. The leather office chair behind it was empty.

"Please, come in, Ms. Chanley." The masculine voice edged with a hint of impatience startled her.

She saw then that the lawyer was sitting on a dark leather couch in a far corner of the room. As he stood up, he put down some folders on an already loaded coffee table. His eyes traveled over her as she walked toward him.

"I'm David Ardell." He introduced himself as if he wasn't certain that she had come to the right office.

"Yes, I know." She felt a smile hover on her lips. He was definitely more attractive in person than on television, even though a slight frown marred his handsome features. "Thank you for seeing me."

What now? David thought. At any other time, he might have enjoyed the interruption of an attractive dark-haired woman, but the governor was waiting for a report that was only half finished, and he had to attend a committee meeting in a few minutes. He caught the waver of a smile and the confident lift of her head as she came toward him. Who was she, anyway? Some socialite wanting him to serve on a community committee as representative of the governor? Then he remembered his secretary had told him that she was a reporter for a local woman's magazine. Great, he thought wryly.

"How can I help you?" he asked, already forming a routine dodge for handling the matter, whatever it was.

"I'm sorry to bother you, Mr. Ardell, but this is important."

That didn't surprise him. Heaven knows, half of
what crossed his desk was stuff *somebody* at the capital thought was urgent and needed his immediate attention. Sometimes he felt like a firefighter with a
dozen fires to put out. "Yes, Ms. Chanley?"

From his tone Melissa knew that he was ready to
get rid of her as quickly as possible. Only the dire
necessity of her visit stiffened her resolve to take as
much time as she needed to make him understand the
situation.

"I'm here at the request of someone else," she said
evenly. "And when you know who, I'm sure you'll
agree that my mission is important enough to take up
a few minutes of your time."

Something in her tone warned David that his intention to dismiss her in short order might be premature. For a moment he let himself appreciate the
way she held her slender shoulders and kept her unbelievable pansy-blue eyes locked on his face. Even
the trim summer suit couldn't hide feminine curves
or lovely long legs showing under a modest-length
skirt as she stood in front of him, her head high, her
eyes fixed directly on his as if she was the one in
control of the situation.

"May I ask who sent you?" David's involvement
in the political world had made him appreciate a wor-
thy adversary. He sensed that in some fashion Melissa
Chanley was here to challenge him.

"This will take a few minutes," she said smoothly.
"Shall we sit down?"

"Of course. I'm sorry." He chuckled to himself at
how deftly she'd taken charge of the interview by that

simple request. Maybe this was going to be interesting, after all. Her firm yet gracious manner was fresh and appealing, and in spite of himself he was intrigued with the reason for her visit. He couldn't ever remember meeting her at any of the political fundraisers or rallies, and he was certain he would not forget a woman as attractive as she.

"Please, sit down." He motioned her to the leather couch and he eased down into a chair opposite her. Moving a few things around on the coffee table, he said, "As you can see I'm trying to dig out from under some paperwork that the governor's office unloaded on me. I'm sorry I don't have time to offer you some coffee. Unfortunately, I have a meeting in a few minutes. Perhaps you'd rather make an appointment on another day when I have more time?"

"No. I'm afraid this can't wait." Melissa's heart began to race. *Speak into my words, Lord. Give me the wisdom I need.*

"All right, Ms. Chanley." He raised a questioning dark brown eyebrow. "I understand that you're a writer for *Women of the West* magazine?" He allowed himself a smile. "I really can't see that I have anything to offer in the way of material for your publication."

"I'm not here in my professional capacity," Melissa explained as she reached into her white leather bag and took out a piece of paper. "I have a message for you from Jolene McCombre."

Jolene McCombre.

He stiffened and for one startling moment he wondered if he'd heard the name correctly, but something in the way Melissa Chanley was looking at him said that there had been no mistake. Just hearing the name jerked the scab off a wound that had never quite healed. Until that moment, he'd thought that he had successfully buried everything having to do with his high school sweetheart.

They had planned to marry as soon as he finished law school, but Jolene had jilted him a month before their wedding, disappeared from his life and married a serviceman who was home on leave. David had never gotten over Jolene's cruel betrayal, and even though some protective instinct warned him not to open that door again, he knew better than to lie about knowing the woman who had left him at the altar.

"You have a message for me from Jolene," he repeated in a tight voice. "What kind of message?"

Melissa fingered the letter in her hand, unsure how she should prepare him for the contents. His expression had become a closed mask, and hardness flickered in the depths of his brown eyes. She knew that the success of her mission depended upon how well she handled the next few minutes. "Before I give you the letter, I want to explain how I got it."

David gave her a noncommittal nod and remained silent. Better not to say anything until he knew exactly why this woman was here and what her intent was. She was a writer, after all. Had Melissa Chanley stumbled into this juicy tidbit of his past and planned to use it for some nefarious purpose of her own? Busy with his life and career, he had lost all track of Jolene through the years. Why would she be sending him a letter through this stranger? A flicker of intuition warned that this meeting was going to challenge his determination to leave the past buried.

"My magazine does profiles on women, past and present, who have shown strength and dedication in a lifetime of helping others," Melissa explained. "I was doing an article on May Bowers who founded the Denver Christian Shelter for homeless women and children. While spending time with May and collecting information for my article, I made friends with some of the women in the shelter, and they shared their stories of abandonment and poverty with me." Melissa drew a firming breath. "Jolene was one of them."

His eyes widened in disbelief. "She was one of the women at the shelter?"

Melissa nodded. "Yes. Penniless and homeless with two little boys. Apparently, the father of the boys died when they were two and three years old, and she raised them by herself until last year when she married a man who took her for everything she had. The scoundrel ended up in prison for fraud, and left her with huge bills and no money. She came to Denver, hoping to find a job and start again, but she became ill before she could find work and ended up at the shelter. I befriended her two little boys, Richie and Eric, and when Jolene was taken to the hospital she asked me to take care of them instead of leaving them at the shelter."

"Is Jolene there now? In the hospital?" When she shook her head, he said, "Oh, I see. You took her home with you." Now, he understood. Ms. Chanley was here to get money from him for Jolene and her kids.

"No, I'm afraid Jolene never made it out of the hospital."

He swallowed hard. "She died?"

"Yes, I'm sorry. She gave me this letter in the hospital, and asked me to read and deliver it if she didn't make it." She handed him the folded sheet of paper.

David's stomach took a sickening plunge as he focused on the familiar handwriting. Jolene had written him every week while he was in law school, and there was no doubt that she had penned this letter. For a moment he wanted to hand the note back without reading it. Then he took himself in hand. He was not the same person he'd been ten years ago.

Melissa watched as David read the letter written by a mother who knew she was dying. Jolene had simply reminded David Ardell of the love they had once shared and asked him to look after her sons now that she was no longer able to care for them. Her greatest fear was that they would end up in foster homes, and she begged David to use his resources to assure their care and happiness.

Melissa searched David's expression as he read it, but his thoughts were hidden from her. Only his long fingers tightening slightly on the letter hinted at an inner turmoil. He was good at hiding his emotions, she thought. Jolene had not shared much about their past relationship, and Melissa only knew what was in the letter.

Slowly he folded the letter, and when he raised his

dark eyes and looked at her, his gaze was guarded and his mouth set in a firm line. "I'll have to check this out, of course."

"Please do. May Bowers and St. Joseph's Hospital can verify everything I've told you. I'm sorry to be the messenger in this situation," she said sincerely, sensing a deep concern beneath his professional demeanor. She suspected that he tried to keep his personal hurts hidden from everyone.

"It isn't that I doubt your integrity," he assured her.

"I understand. Anyone in your prominent position has to be careful. You can check out the handwriting with May."

"That won't be necessary, but there are some other things that I want to verify. Where are the boys now?"

"They are still with me."

"And how old are they?"

"Eric is six, and Richie is almost five. They're very bright little boys." She smiled. "Most of the time, they're pretty easy to handle."

"Unfortunately, it may take a little time to track down any relatives who could take them, but I'll put an investigator on it right away." David had recovered from his initial shock, and his agile mind had begun to search for ways to handle the situation with impersonal dispatch. If things were exactly as she had told him, he didn't have much choice but to get involved, temporarily at least.

"I hope we can find someone soon. We need to get the boys settled as soon as possible."

"I know that Jolene's parents passed away some years ago—and I know nothing about the father's relatives," he added with a hard edge in his tone, referring to the man Jolene had chosen to marry. "Did she make any mention of family while she was at the shelter?"

"No, and I doubt that she would have been there with her children if she'd had any family to go to," Melissa said. "I took the boys because there was no one else she could ask."

"I see, and you're willing to keep them until some other arrangements have been made?" He used a professional lawyer tone, as if he were taking a deposition instead of handling a very personal matter. He did not want to meet the children that under different circumstances might have been his.

"No, I'm afraid not. I'm not in any position to keep Eric and Richie at my place," she said firmly. Where was a sign of compassion for the woman he had once intended to marry?

"If it's a matter of monetary compensation, I'm sure we can come to some satisfactory arrangement. I'm willing to assume the expenses of the children's care while you have them."

"How generous of you," she said with gravel in her voice. Obviously, his checkbook was as close as he intended to get to the sweet little boys who could use a caring man in their lives right now.

"You should be compensated in some fashion for their care," he said, well aware of the sarcasm in her tone. A flash of anger in her lovely blue eyes startled him. She looked ready to light into him. What was the matter? His offer seemed reasonable enough. Was she after more money than just expenses for keeping the boys? "Did you have some specific arrangement in mind?"

"Although I would love to keep Eric and Richie, I can't. And it isn't a matter of compensation." She didn't want him to think she was trying to fleece him out of any money for keeping them. "I live in a studio basement apartment with a fold-down bed. We've been playing camping with sleeping bags. I've managed to keep Eric and Richie fairly entertained in the small space, but some other accommodations have to be made." She eyed him frankly. "What kind of living space do you have?"

He knew the question was rhetorical. From the thrust of her chin, he could tell that she already knew from reading the society pages that he lived in Denver's fashionable Cherry Creek district in a spacious family home, which was his residence now that his parents had retired and moved to Florida. He decided to deliberately sidestep the inference that he had a home large enough to comfortably house the two boys.

"Frankly, I'm not quite sure what Jolene expected me to do in this situation." There was no way that he was going to become personally responsible for the care of Jolene's two boys. He'd do his best to find a relative to take them, and he'd foot the bill for their care until then. That was it.

"I think it's pretty clear that she wanted you to look after them, Mr. Ardell."

"It's David," he said, brushing away her formality. "And I will do my best to get them placed."

Melissa looked at him with a warning in her large eyes. If he suggested they call Children's Services to take the children, she was ready to challenge that decision. "We need to do what's best for the children."

"Yes, of course, but we have to consider what would be better for them in the long run. Don't we, Melissa?"

"The long run," she echoed in disbelief. "You and I have the responsibility of deciding what should happen to them right now, today. We have two little boys that have just lost their mother. Sadly enough, their lives have been in a state of upheaval almost since the day they were born." What they need is someone to love and take care of them now!

"What options do we have?" David didn't like the feeling that she was personally attacking him. None of this was of his making. He sympathized with the homeless little boys and regretted that Jolene had made such a mess of her life, but the responsibility for the situation was not his. "My taking on the personal care of two youngsters is impossible."

"Surely you know a nice family with children who would take Eric and Richie until a relative can be located," Melissa insisted, knowing she had lost the first round. He wasn't going to get personally involved.

"Honestly, I don't." He brushed back a forelock of dark blond hair and frowned. "My single life doesn't include anyone close enough that I can call up and dump two strange kids on them. If you could just keep them temporarily—''

''I told you I don't have the space. I wish I did, but I don't. This afternoon I had to leave Eric and Richie with my landlady, whose apartment is almost as small as mine.'' She refrained from telling him that the past two weeks had been an almost impossible challenge—trying to meet her deadlines at the various magazines she wrote for, while cooped up in a basement apartment scarcely big enough for one adult, let alone two rambunctious little boys. She fell silent, waiting for him to decide what he was going to do about Jolene's request—if anything.

He was silent for a moment, then he asked, ''And what about time?''

She looked puzzled. ''What do you mean?''

''Have you had the time to care for them?''

''I've made the time,'' she said flatly. ''Since I'm a freelance writer, I can set my own work hours. That's the only way I've been able to spend days at the park with the boys, and compose at night with my laptop computer on the kitchen table.''

''I see.'' He surprised her by suddenly getting up from his chair and easing down beside her on the couch. ''Well, Melissa, we may have a solution, after all.''

She caught a whiff of spicy men's cologne as she steadied herself against his nearness. *Careful,* she warned herself. David Ardell's ability to deftly manage people was evident in the disarming smile he gave her.

''Let's look at the problem this way. You have the

time to care for the children but not the space. I have the space but no one to care for the children. Doesn't the answer seem obvious?'' He raised a questioning eyebrow.

"What are you suggesting?"

"A businesslike solution. While I hire an investigator to find the boys' relatives, you could move into my house temporarily to care for them."

"I couldn't do that," she said quickly. "Move in with you, like that. It wouldn't be proper."

"You wouldn't be moving in with me." David was amused by the indignant spark in her eyes. Her reaction told him a great deal about her moral fiber, and he hastened to reassure her that his offer was strictly based on the children's welfare. "This arrangement would have nothing to do with me, no more than if I hired you as a live-in nanny for the children. And I'm willing to do that, make it purely a business arrangement. Just consider it a temporary job until this thing is settled. You can still keep up your obligations at the magazines. I think it's a perfect solution all around."

"I don't know. It seems very…irregular."

He saw a flicker of indecision in her eyes. "You don't have to be afraid that you'll have to suffer my company," he assured her. "I'm rarely at home. Believe me, we would scarcely see each other."

When she remained silent, obviously weighing what he was saying, he stressed the point that the arrangement would be a good one for Eric and Richie. "The place is large enough for you and the boys to be perfectly comfortable staying there. There's a lovely fenced-in backyard with plenty of grass for running and jumping. You could even set up your work on the covered patio while the boys are playing."

Melissa found the idea of living in a place that must be ten times bigger than any place she'd ever had, to be a little frightening. "And we would be alone in the house, except when you're there?"

"No, I have a wonderful couple, Inga and Hans Erickson, who take care of the cooking and housekeeping. They've been with my family since I was in grade school, and they'll be delighted to have some youngsters in the house." Inga was always lamenting the fact that David wasn't married and raising his own children by now. "You'll like them. And I'll bet they'll like you."

Melissa hesitated. The offer was unconventional, to say the least. She had hoped that David would respond to Jolene's request and see to the boys' care, but she hadn't expected to be part of the package.

Was this the answer she had been praying for? Would it be the best arrangement for Eric and Richie? She had already grown so fond of them. She knew she couldn't have the boys permanently, but turning them over to strangers pulled at her heartstrings. The possibility of keeping them in her life a little longer was tempting.

"Well, what do you think?" David asked, surprised at how much he wanted her to say yes.

"How long do you think it will be before we find the right place for the boys? And will the authorities let us keep them until we do?"

"I can take care of all the legal matters. That's no problem. We'll just have to wait and see what an investigator turns up and then decide our next step." He smiled. "Maybe I ought to give you time to think about it."

"I don't see any better solution at the moment," she said honestly. Eric and Richie deserved to live in a nice place for a change. Some of things they said about being hungry and cold when they were home-less made her grateful that they'd have the chance to live in a nice home and play outside in the beautiful Colorado summer weather.

"All right." She was taking a leap of faith that she was doing the right thing. "We'll consider it a nanny job with no pay except board and room for the three of us," she said firmly. She'd spent one summer as a hired companion to a disabled little girl, and this situation wouldn't be much different—if David Ardell kept his distance as promised. "I'll stay at your house with the children until your investigator locates some relatives and we find a proper home for them."

"Good. It's a deal," he said. "When do you want to move in?"

"Tomorrow morning. I'll need the rest of the day to make arrangements for the move."

"Fine." He suddenly realized that having her around would be a definite boost to his lonely life—then he caught himself. He'd promised her that he would make himself scarce if she moved into the house. Now, as he looked into her soft blue eyes and at her appealing smile, he realized that it might be the hardest promise he'd ever had to keep.

Chapter Two

Melissa's heart sank as she viewed the spacious white brick mansion and beautifully landscaped grounds set back from the road. What business did she and two rambunctious youngsters have living in a place like that?

"Are we lost?" Eric asked with childish anxiety as he sat stiffly beside her in the front seat. The large brown eyes in his thin, pinched face were filled with apprehension. He was a small-boned child and terribly underweight. Wiry sandy hair hung longish over his ears and narrow forehead, and freckles dotted his slender nose.

"No, we're not lost," she quickly assured him as she turned into the curved driveway that led to the front of the house. The upheavals of Eric's young life had already left its mark. He had just begun to trust Melissa and was opening up a little to her. Guarded and solemn, the young boy was the protector of his little brother, who was sitting in the back seat happily munching a fruit bar.

"This is Mr. Ardell's house. It's pretty, isn't it?" she said brightly as she braked in front of marble steps leading up to a terraced veranda and double wooden doors with etched glass windows.

"Are we going to stay here a long time?"

A long time? She knew what Eric was really asking. *Is this home?* She hated to think about how many times the small boys had moved around before they ended up at the homeless shelter.

"We're going to stay here until we find someone in your mommy's or daddy's family who want you two lovely boys to come and live with them," she said brightly. "Then you won't have to move anymore."

"What if we don't find anybody?"

"We will. You wait and see." *Ask and it shall be given, seek and ye shall find.* Never had the scripture seemed more reassuring than it did in this situation. The grandmother who had raised Melissa had lived by that promise, and her faith in God's guidance had been instilled in Melissa from an early age.

"But what if they don't like us?" Eric insisted with childish pugnaciousness. "Some people don't like kids."

"Maybe not, but I know they would love you and Richie." Impulsively, Melissa gave him a quick hug, and was rewarded with a weak smile. "Now, let's unload our stuff and see what the inside of this place looks like. I bet you guys won't have to sleep on the floor anymore. How about that?"

"Goody," Richie said with a four-year-old's enthusiasm. He had a mop of dark brown hair, a bone structure that was heavier than his sandy-haired brother's and the same large dark eyes. "I want a bed—a big, big bed." Then he giggled as if a thought tickled him. "And I'm going to jump up and down on it lots."

"No, you're not," Melissa corrected quickly, trying to blot out a picture of two playful boys turning some elegant bed into a trampoline. "There'll be a nice backyard for you to play in. Now, let's get out of the car and take a look at this place."

She hoped they couldn't see her nervousness as they unloaded the trunk and set the luggage on the front step. The pile included only two small suitcases, her laptop computer and a brown sack containing a book and old baseball that Eric wouldn't let out of his sight.

The boys had few clothes, and they were wearing the one new outfit of jeans and summer shirts that Melissa had bought them. She'd return to her place to pick up things for herself if their stay lasted more than a week.

When she'd talked to David last night and arranged to arrive about ten o'clock in the morning, he told her that Inga and Hans Erickson would help them settle in. He also assured her that an excellent investigator in Denver had agreed to conduct a search. The man expected to have something to report within ten days.

Ten days.

As they stood at the elegant front door and waited

for someone to answer the bell, Melissa had the feeling that ten days could be a lifetime.

"Maybe nobody's home," Eric said with his usual worried expression. Before Melissa could stop Richie, he reached up and pushed the button a half-dozen times.

"Don't, Richie." She pulled his hand away, just as the door swung open. David stood there, a slight frown on his handsome face.

"The doorbell works," he said wryly.

"I'm sorry, Richie got carried away," she apologized. Great, she thought. Off to a great start. David was obviously on his way out, in a beige business suit that did great things for his dark blond hair and tanned complexion.

"Usually Inga answers the door, but she's busy in the kitchen and I was just leaving," he explained. "Come on in. Hans will bring your luggage." He opened the door wide and stepped back.

Melissa motioned the boys to go in ahead of her. Richie bounced through the door with his usual childish eagerness, and Eric followed more slowly, hugging a brown paper sack as if it were his only anchor in a threatening world.

"Say hello to Mr. Ardell, boys," Melissa prompted, but when neither responded, she said quickly, "This is Eric."

David smiled at him. "I'm glad to meet you, Eric." The solemn-faced little boy only nodded slightly.

"Richie, say hello to Mr. Ardell," Melissa said, but a black glass fountain in the middle of the spacious foyer had already caught the little boy's attention.

Ignoring everyone, Richie bounding over to it, squatted down and stared into the pool of water. Then he looked up at David with a frown. "No fish?"

"No fish," David echoed.

"Did you already eat them?"

The humor in the innocent question was tempered by the child's honest bewilderment, and David held back a laugh as he shook his head. "No. I don't think real fish would like a little pond like that."

"Not like a big, big lake," Richie agreed solemnly, and then, before Melissa could react, his little hand picked up one of the colorful pebbles decorating the fountain display. He threw the rock so hard that it made a resounding splash in the water against the glass bottom.

"Richie!" Melissa gasped.

Dear God, no. They had been in the house less than five minutes, and already...disaster.

David grabbed Richie's arm before he could pick up another pebble. He jerked the boy back from the fountain and said harshly, "No! Don't throw rocks. Understand?"

Richie let out a frightened whimper, and Eric's normal passiveness shattered. Fiery color rose in his freckled face, and he threw himself at David. His little fists pounded David. "Let my brother go!"

"Eric! Eric, stop it." Melissa pulled him back and held his arms firmly. "No one's going to hurt Richie."

At that moment, she felt cold water easing into her

open-toed summer sandals and knew her worst fear
was realized. The rock had cracked the glass pool,
and water was leaking out on the foyer floor.

She heard someone in the doorway behind her draw
in a breath. Melissa turned and saw a large-boned
woman with a round face, yellow hair braided in a
coronet around the top of her head and blue eyes widened in disbelief. ''What is going on?'' she demanded
with a slight Swedish accent.

Richie wiggled away from David and ran to Melissa. She stood there with both boys hugging her, not
knowing what to say to David or the housekeeper.

''The fountain is leaking,'' David said shortly.
''Get Hans.''

The woman nodded, gave one last look at the growing pool of water in the middle of the foyer, turned
on her heel and left, muttering something under her
breath.

''I am so sorry,'' Melissa said. ''Richie didn't
mean any harm.''

David started to say something, but seeing her
standing there, defensive and ready to meet his anger
with the protectiveness of a mother bear defending
her cubs, and two boys glaring at him as if he were
some kind of ogre, he couldn't find the right words.
He swallowed back the urge to launch into a lecture
about proper behavior while under his roof. At the
moment, he would rather have addressed a belligerent
jury than his houseguests. He finally settled for a
brisk, ''We'll talk tonight.''

Melissa nodded, and her hands tightened on the
boys' shoulders in a reassuring squeeze. She could

feel the tremors in their little bodies as they hugged her sides.

"Inga will help you get settled. She's prepared two adjoining bedrooms on the second floor, and there's a small lady's parlor off the breakfast room that you can use as a working office. If the arrangements are not satisfactory, let me know and we'll work out something else."

"I'm sure they'll be fine," she answered in the same businesslike tone, trying to ignore the widening spread of water about to reach his expensive, polished shoes.

"Well, then, I have to get to the office." He glanced once more at the draining pool, wondering how many more catastrophes two little boys could create in the space of a few days.

Melissa saw his frown. "I'll keep a close rein on the boys," she promised.

As he nodded and turned toward the door, his shoes squeaked wetly with each step, and she wondered if the governor's counselor was going to work with damp socks. Melissa put a hand up to her mouth and suppressed a giggle.

When Inga returned with Hans and his mopping equipment, she indicated that they were to follow her, and led the way into a spacious front hall. It was obvious that the house was a decorator's dream, a fact that Inga didn't hesitate to point out. "This house is filled with nice things. *Very* nice things."

"It is lovely," Melissa agreed as she glimpsed beautifully furnished rooms opening off the main corridor. She felt as if she were someone viewing a showcase home, instead of someone who was about to be a resident in such luxurious surroundings.

Holding tightly to the boys' hands, she followed the housekeeper up a wide central staircase. A massive grandfather clock on the landing chimed the hour just as they passed it. Startled, both Eric and Richie missed the next step, stopped and stared at the clock in wonder.

Melissa smiled at their wide, rounded eyes. Obviously the boys had never heard anything like the resonant Westminster chimes. They begged to wait and hear the clock again, but Melissa shook her head, promising that it would chime many more times while they were there.

"Mr. David said to put you in the front bedrooms," Inga said in a tone that indicated it wouldn't have been her choice for the temporary houseguests.

Nor mine, Melissa thought as they accompanied Inga down the hall to the front of the house. The size and fashionable decor of the two front bedrooms made ready for her and the boys was unbelievable. Her room alone had more living space than her small studio apartment, and the boys' bedroom was only slightly smaller. Even Eric and Richie were subdued by surroundings that were completely alien to their experience. Both boys stayed close to Melissa as if she were some kind of life preserver, as they walked through the bedrooms and peeked into the large adjoining bathroom.

"Very nice," Melissa said, nodding her approval. She wasn't about to show any uneasiness or awkwardness, but she knew that Inga was wondering why a temporary nanny was being given one of the best rooms in the house. Melissa couldn't help but wonder the same thing. She would have been much more comfortable with accommodations in line with those of Inga and Hans.

The housekeeper's manners had softened when she realized the little boys weren't going to turn into hooligans. "Mr. David said you are to use his mother's sitting room for your work," Inga told Melissa. "He didn't say what kind of work."

"I'm a writer for a magazine, and I can set up my small computer anywhere. I really don't need a special room." She glanced around the bedroom and failed to see anything that might serve as a desk, but she wasn't about to ask Inga or Hans to start moving in furniture. "Thank you, Mrs. Erickson, for your help—"

"Inga," she corrected.

Melissa held out her hand. "Nice to meet you, Inga. And I'm Melissa."

A softness touched the woman's blue eyes. "Melissa. Pretty name. Mr. David says it is a nice thing you are doing, taking care of the children. You are a good lady." Then she eyed Richie and Eric. "And they are good boys, ya?"

"Yes, they are very good boys," Melissa echoed, smiling at the obvious combination of question and warning in Inga's tone.

Just then, her husband came in with the small suitcases and Melissa's computer. Hans Erickson was a broad-faced man with huge shoulders, thick arms and brown hair lightly highlighted with gray. He just nod-

ded at Melissa when she thanked him for bringing up
the luggage.

"I'm sorry about the fountain," she told him. "It
was just an accident. Richie didn't mean to break it."

"I know. He's a good boy. I can tell that." He
smiled down at Richie. "Mr. David give you a bad
time? You ask him about throwing a rock through the
kitchen window, eh?" He winked at Melissa and then
walked out of the room, chuckling.

"Boys," Inga said with undisguised fondness in
her smile. "They never grow up."

Melissa laughed, suddenly feeling that Hans and
Inga had given them a pardon for the fountain inci-
dent. Maybe David would have second thoughts
about the whole thing, and they could start again on
a harmonious footing.

It took all of ten minutes to "settle in." The beds
in the boys' room were twins. Eric seemed satisfied,
but Richie ignored the beds and immediately scrambled up in the middle of Melissa's queen size bed.

"No jumping," she warned him. From the sparkle
in his eyes, she suspected the first time she turned her
back, he'd get on his knees and bounce.

Her stomach tightened. How could she keep them
corralled in this fashion-plate house? There wasn't
anything in the two bedrooms that would keep the
boys occupied and happy, and the few things she'd
brought like crayons and coloring books wouldn't last
for very long.

Somehow, in some way, she had to make the next
few days a comforting and healing time for the boys.

* * *

"No doubt about it, you're the governor's fair-haired boy," Stella Day told David with a pleased smile as they lunched at Denver's fashionable Cherry Creek Country Club. "We all know he's schooling you for big things. If you keep focused, you've got a wonderful future ahead of you, David."

He was pleased with this optimistic projection from the governor's executive assistant, but he knew he had a long way to go. "Right now, I'm just learning the ins and outs of government."

"Well, your father and mother are going to be very proud of you one of these elections when you run for Colorado's attorney general."

David knew that his parents held high expectations of him. He was used to the pressure they'd put on him as he was growing up. As their only child, there was never any question about David following in their footsteps. His father had been a state senator until he retired, and his mother had been a political activist. It was clearly due to their influence that the governor was promoting David's legal career, and they were expecting him to make his mark in politics.

"It's a little premature to think anything like that," he answered evenly, and turned the conversation back to the business that had brought them together. David was used to these working lunches. In fact, he couldn't remember very many meals when he wasn't conducting some kind of business for the governor.

Stella had an appointment waiting for her right after lunch, so she didn't tarry. After she drove away in her car, David sat for a moment in his luxurious sedan, trying to make a decision about whether to drop by his house since he was so close, or head back to his office downtown.

He hated to admit it, but he hadn't been able to put the morning's fiasco out of his mind. A nagging sense of guilt plagued him when he remembered Richie's frightened face and Melissa's eyes sparking fire.

Better mend some fences, he decided as he drove out of the parking lot. Even though he'd probably be a little late for his afternoon appointments, he wanted to swing by the house for a few minutes and try to set things right. He didn't want Melissa Chanley upset with him. Something about her steady, totally feminine, and yet uncompromising personality challenged him. Even dressed as she had been that morning in jeans and a simple white pullover, she could hold her own with any of the stylishly dressed women who had lunched at the club. She intrigued him, and he knew that if the boys didn't accept him, it wasn't likely that she would, either.

He parked his car at the house and was about to enter a side door, when squeals and laughter coming from the backyard stopped him. Curious, he walked down the narrow sidewalk, opened the gate and came around the back of the house.

Then he stopped short. "What in the world?"

Both boys and Melissa were on the ground, rolling over and over down a grassy incline that led away from a terraced patio. When they reached the bottom of the slope, they ran back to the top and, shouting and giggling, started rolling down again.

The boys always beat Melissa to the bottom and sat up, squealing, "You lose. You lose."

Melissa laughed as she pulled dry grass from her tousled hair. "All right. I give up." Then she glanced up and saw David standing a few feet away. The expression on his face was one of incredulity.

As she got to her feet, her first impulse was to give in to total embarrassment. Instead, she managed a smile and gave him an airy wave of her hand. "Hi, there. Would you like to enter our contest? The Best Roller Down the Hill?"

At first, he didn't answer, then he surprised Melissa by returning her smile. "I might. What are the prizes?"

"There aren't any," Eric said flatly. Both boys had moved to Melissa's side and were glaring at him as if he had no right to intrude upon their fun.

"Well, I guess I'll pass, then," David said. "Maybe I'll join you in a different game sometime."

"Nothing else to play." Richie scowled at him.

"He doesn't have kids' stuff because he doesn't like them," Eric told his brother with his usual solemnity.

Melissa didn't look at David's face, and held back from saying anything. She hadn't found anything in the house that would keep two lively boys happy and occupied. Now she sensed an instant tightening in David's body as he stood beside her, but it wasn't her place to correct the boys. Maybe Eric told the truth. Maybe David didn't like kids. It was hard to tell about things like that, and his beautiful home and lifestyle didn't give a clue. In fact, she hadn't seen any evi-

dence during her earlier tour of the house that the
young boy he had once been had ever lived here.

"Maybe we can find some stuff for you, boys,"
David said, ignoring the remark about his not liking
kids. He'd been too busy in the world of lawyers and
politicians to know whether the remark was closer to
the truth than he was willing to admit.

"That would be nice, wouldn't it, boys?" Melissa
said, but their expressions didn't change.

"Sorry, I have to run. I just dropped by to see if
Inga and Hans were being helpful," he lied. He knew
the Swedish couple would rally to the cause, no matter how much extra work it created.

"Oh, yes, they're wonderful. Inga fixed us a nice
lunch, and the boys ate every bit of it."

"Good. And you've found working space?"

"The small sitting room will be fine. It's lovely
with the windows overlooking the garden." She knew
the sitting room had been his mother's, and Melissa
was curious about the woman who had raised such a
purposeful, solitary son.

"I have a late meeting tonight so I'll have dinner
in town. If you need to reach me, tell Inga and she'll
pass the message along." He turned to say something
to the boys, but his usually articulate tongue failed
him. All he could come up with was a quick "So
long. See you guys later."

Later that afternoon, the boys were down for a nap
when the delivery truck arrived with a bright red
swing set, jungle gym and small merry-go-round.

Melissa was working in the sitting room when she
saw Hans and another man setting up the playground

equipment in the backyard. Who would believe it? David must have stopped at a store on his way back to the office, bought everything and paid extra to have it delivered that very afternoon.

She was delighted, and totally surprised. Maybe he was bent on hiding from everyone what a softy he really was.

She remembered how he'd smiled at her as she sat on the ground with blades of grass caught in her hair. Why had he come back to the house? He'd warned her that he would hardly ever be around, but he had been here when they arrived this morning and he had shown up again after lunch. Even though she was pleased by his attention, she wasn't comfortable with it. Maybe this whole arrangement had been a big mistake, she thought—until she reminded herself that this was the perfect place for the boys until the right home was found for them. She knew that Eric and Richie would be ecstatic with the playground equipment, and she was relieved that the boys could play outside, while she worked and kept an eye on them through the sitting room windows. The only sad part about the gift was that it would never replace the male companionship David could have given them.

Chapter Three

"Burning the midnight oil, are you?" David teased later that evening as he leaned up against the door frame of the sitting room and smiled at her.

"Just a little." She saw that his tie hung loosely, his white shirt was wrinkled, and he was carrying his summer jacket. "You look as if you've had a full day."

"It's been a long one. How did things go with you? Did the play stuff get here?" He walked over to the back window and squinted out into the night. Decorative patio floodlights spilled out into the yard, and she could tell that he was satisfied by what he saw.

"Yes, they're great. The boys loved everything. Especially the jungle gym. You should have seen them. They looked like a couple of monkeys, climbing and swinging—and scaring the daylights out of me." She laughed. "They're working up some tricks to show you."

The tired lines in his face eased. "Really? I mean,

after that little episode this morning I thought I rated number one Grinch.''

"Children are very adaptive and forgiving, if you give them a chance." She almost added that they were great teachers, too. She suspected that David could learn a lot about himself if he spent a little time with Eric and Richie while they were here.

"I'm sorry I reacted so strongly about the fountain. It's just that it was one of the things that my mother prized, and I felt protective of it."

"I understand. You have a lovely house, and the boys need to respect that. Thank you for taking them in while we find someone who will give them a good home." She got up from the desk. "Well, I think I'll call it a day. How about you?"

He sighed. "I have some briefs to look over, and I'd best get started. Of course, you could agree to try some of my famous hot chocolate and give me an excuse to procrastinate a little longer."

An automatic refusal was on her lips. "No telling how early the boys will be up and about. I really should get to bed."

He nodded, as if he had expected her refusal. "Yes, of course. Good night, then."

Somehow she sensed that his brisk tone was protective and a cover-up for lonely feelings he didn't want her to see. His obvious need to talk with someone touched her.

"Come to think of it, a warm drink does sound good," she mused. "Maybe I'll change my mind. That's a woman's prerogative, you know." She laughed and met his steady dark eyes.

"So I've been told." David smiled. He liked the way she was able to change her mind without any long drawn-out justification. She seemed to be perfectly at ease with herself, and he realized that there was no need for him to play a role or keep his guard up when he was with her. "Come on, then. We'll mess up Inga's kitchen and get bawled out for it in the morning."

He led the way into the kitchen, and Melissa perched on a high stool at the breakfast counter while he prepared the cocoa. A shock of hair drifted across his forehead, and his rumpled appearance made him seem less formidable than usual. She wondered if he ever relaxed enough to wear something comfortable, like jeans and knit shirts.

She was surprised at how efficient he was in the kitchen. He had two steaming cups of hot chocolate ready in no time, and sat on the stool beside her as they sipped the hot drink.

"Mmm, delicious. You're a man of many talents, I see."

"Hot chocolate is about the peak of my culinary art," he admitted. "And now that I've revealed my hidden expertise in the kitchen, it's your turn. What secret talents are you hiding from the world?"

She laughed. "No secrets. My life is an open book, but that's not the one I want to write." She hadn't intended to talk about the goal she had set for herself, but the way he was looking at her invited an explanation. "Since I've been writing for the magazine, I've run into some wonderful accounts of strong, spiritual women who helped settle the Rocky Mountain west. I'm trying to organize their stories in a book. I started it before my grandmother died, almost three years ago. She was the one who raised me after my parents died in a car accident when I was eight years old. She told me true stories about courageous women who held on to Christian values while they raised families in wild, frontier towns. I was fascinated by their devotion to family values and faith in God, and I decided to write a book about them.''

"Well, if you believe in something, I guess you should do it,'' he said. It wasn't an enthusiastic endorsement.

His tone left Melissa wondering why she was sharing her passion with this man who probably thought she was some dewy-eyed female, wasting her talents on a book that would have limited marketing appeal. "I don't expect to make a lot of money at it.''

"And are you happy writing for your magazines?''

She nodded, a little piqued that he had been less than encouraging about her book. "Are you happy working for the governor?''

"Sometimes. On the whole, he's a pretty good boss.''

The way he said it, she knew that professional ethics would keep him from discussing his real feelings. Anyway, it wasn't any of her business. "Do you like being an attorney?''

"Most of the time, but trying to find a way through all the legal mazes isn't always rewarding. Sometimes I think law is like looking for a black cat in a dark room.'' He smiled wryly. "You know it's there, but you can't find it.''

"If you weren't an attorney, what would you be?"

He shrugged. "Frankly, I've never given that possibility a thought."

"Not even when you were a little boy?"

"Truthfully, I can't remember back that far. It seems to me that my name was submitted to the University of Denver Law School when I was born." He laughed but there was no mirth in it.

Melissa resisted the temptation to ask about his parents and his boyhood. Prying into his personal life was out of order. He'd made it clear that he was willing to offer the use of his house for a few days, but that didn't include delving into his personal history.

She quickly finished her drink and slipped off the stool. "Thanks for the cocoa. I'm ready to hit the pillow and get prepared for my cherubs tomorrow. Thanks again for the playground equipment. It will make the next few days much easier."

He walked with her to the kitchen door. "I'll call Mr. Weiss, the investigator, tomorrow. Maybe he's turned up something and we can get the boys placed in quick order. Then things will get back to normal."

"We'll try to keep out of your way," she said firmly. His tone had made it clear that he was ready to have them gone as soon as possible. "With luck, we won't overstay our welcome."

"I just meant that it can't be easy for you or the children to be in limbo like this," he added quickly, apparently recognizing he'd said the wrong thing.

"I agree it's important that we get the children settled as soon as possible."

He wanted to tell her how much he'd enjoyed her

company this evening. Her candor and natural manner were refreshing. There was nothing pretentious or false about her, and she allowed him to drop the mask he wore most of the time. If he hadn't promised to stay his distance from her, he would have confessed that he was looking forward to more of her company.

"Let me know if there's anything else that will make your stay more comfortable. I'm going to be gone for a couple days. The governor is scheduled for several events in eastern Colorado and wants me to go along. We'll fly out tomorrow. The Ericksons know how to get in touch with me if something comes up. Just make yourselves at home, please."

She knew that he was doing his best to make things go as smoothly as possible for her and the boys. Having two kids like Eric and Richie running riot in a beautiful home like this would test anyone's Christian charity.

"We'll behave like guests whether you are here or not," she assured him. "Don't worry. Everything will be in one piece when you get back, I promise. Have a safe trip."

He smiled at her. "Thank you. I can't remember the last time someone said that to me."

She turned away quickly, sensing something in the situation that could pull them across the line they'd drawn between them.

David left early the next day, and while he was gone the boys settled into a routine of outdoor play, naps and quiet time. Melissa finished two articles and put them in the mail to her magazine editor. She liked to write two months ahead on her assignments, which gave her some leeway to research her book. There were moments when the uncertainty of the boys' future worried her, but she firmly lectured herself: "Let go and let God." Everything was in His hands. *Lord, give me patience,* she prayed, and then added with a chuckle, "And, please, give it to me right now."

Inga seemed happy to have her company when she popped in the kitchen for a cup of tea. The housekeeper liked to chat, and Melissa's curiosity was satisfied by some of the stories Inga told her about David, his parents and their hope that he would be governor someday.

David leaned back in his seat as the governor's private plane climbed into the air and headed northeast. They were scheduled to arrive in Denver about four o'clock, and the cabin was filled with tired members of the governor's staff. They had been on the go for two days, and David had a briefcase filled with more work when he got back. Not tonight, he thought, anticipating getting home before dark for a change.

"David, I'm handling the reservations for next week's fund-raiser," Stella Day said as she stopped beside his seat with a pencil and pad in her hand. "We need to know how many tables to reserve for the governor's staff. I'm putting you down for two places."

"Two?" David raised an eyebrow, but he knew what was coming. His unattached status was never overlooked when it came to these political affairs.

"The governor wants you to escort the daughter of

one of the speakers. Not bad-looking, I hear. Should be more of a pleasure than a chore,'' Stella promised.

''Sorry, I've already asked someone,'' he lied, deciding that when he showed up alone, he could say the lady had been indisposed. ''You'll have to find another escort to do the honors.''

''Who is she?''

''You don't know her.''

Stella studied him. ''You're lying, David.''

''Am I?'' he asked with a challenging smile.

She let out an exasperated breath. ''You know how important these contacts are. An eligible bachelor like you should venture out of that shell you've put around yourself and start dating. I could give you a list of charming eligible women a mile long. Why don't you let yourself go? Get out and do some socializing?''

''I don't have time,'' David said flatly.

''Make time,'' Stella told him, and walked away sighing.

He knew he'd have to attend the elegant affair, which was to be held at one of Denver's fashionable hotels. Stella was right: it wouldn't sit well if he showed up alone when the governor wanted him to escort another lady. David didn't know when the idea struck him to ask Melissa to be his date, but almost immediately he dismissed it. Of course she'd refuse. She'd hesitated even to move into his house until he'd made it clear that he would hardly be around. Still, the prospect of spending an evening with her kept nagging at him. He didn't doubt for a moment that she would be a delightful dinner partner and could hold her own conversationally with anyone at the table.

By the time the plane landed and he drove home, he had decided to wait a few days before mentioning the social affair. In the meantime, he'd try to get more involved with the boys, a sure way to win her approval.

His good intentions were almost immediately reduced to ashes, when he came into a small utility room off the garage and nearly tripped over a mangy, flea-bitten, stray dog. The mutt was as startled as David. He lurched up on skinny legs, peered at him with round dark eyes through a tangle of dirty brown hair, and backed away from David, barking and growling.

Eric and Richie came bursting through a door that led to the back hall. "Scruffy! Scruffy!" Falling to their knees beside the straggly, long-haired dog, they engulfed him in a protective hug and glared up at David.

As Melissa hurried into the room, David demanded in a sharp tone, "Explain this, please."

She moistened her lips. "I'll try. Boys, go outside with the dog for a little while."

"He's ours," Richie yelled at David.

"We adopted him," Eric added fervently. "He's like us. He ain't got a home."

Melissa didn't look at David as she scooted the boys and the dog into the backyard. She knew that her weakness over the stray dog was going to create friction all the way around. Obviously, David was going to put his foot down about keeping the mutt, and the boys didn't need one more heartbreak in their young lives. She silently prayed for the right words as she went back inside the house to face a glowering David.

He was in the kitchen with Inga, and she was talking to him about dinner. "I baked some stuffed pork chops and potatoes, just in case you made it home in time to eat. The kind of meals you have at those political junkets of yours don't fill up a man the way they should."

"Actually I'm not all that hungry," he said, allowing a wave of weariness to sweep over him. It had been an exhausting trip and all he wanted was to come home to some peace and quiet. He had already decided to put off the confrontation about the dog until later when his nerves weren't so raw. He liked to handle problems in a detached way, and he felt anything but detached about keeping a mangy stray dog—boys, or no boys!

"Why don't you go upstairs and freshen up," Inga coaxed like a mother hen. "I can set the dining room table for you and Melissa, and feed Eric and Richie in the kitchen. Both of you look as if you could use some quiet time. And you need to settle this dog thing, ya?"

David allowed himself a weak smile. "Ya."

"Good. Now, out of my kitchen, both of you. Dinner in half an hour."

David and Melissa exchanged smiles as Inga banished them from her kitchen.

When David came downstairs, he was surprised to see Melissa already seated at the dining room table.

She had changed into a simple pink dress revealing her tanned arms and shoulders, and her raven-dark hair glistened in the soft light from an overhead chandelier. She looked lovely. Pleasure sluiced through him and his evening took a brighter turn as he looked at her.

"Sorry to keep you waiting," he said quickly, taking a chair opposite her.

"You didn't. I was trying to get the boys settled in the kitchen, and Inga ordered me out." Melissa laughed.

"Inga insisted they eat with her and Hans tonight. She put Hans at the table between them, so I guess everything's under control."

"We can always hope," he said dryly, and then quickly changed the subject. He wasn't ready to spoil the evening so soon. The subject of the dog could wait a while, but there was no "question" in his mind about it—the dog had to go.

"How is the writing coming?" he asked politely.

As they talked for a few minutes about her current assignment, she realized what a polished dinner companion he was. He kept the conversation moving, asking questions and listening to her answers with a soft smile on his face.

As he leaned toward her, his slightly damp hair was burnished by the light's glow into shades of golden brown. He wore tailored brown slacks and an expensive chambray shirt open at the neck.

"I decided to go freelance because I felt called to write my women's book," she told him as she reached for a crystal water glass and took a sip.

"'Called'?" He raised a skeptical eyebrow. "That's an interesting word."

"Yes, I believe that there is a divine pattern in our lives. If we will only let go and let God, surprising things will happen. Haven't you ever felt that a coincidence is not that at all?"

Inga's entrance with a loaded tray saved him from getting into any discussion of her naive beliefs. As he looked at her, Melissa's eyes were sparkling with such sincerity, he didn't have the heart to argue that it was up to an individual to make things happen in his or her life, not some far-off deity.

As expected, the meal was delicious, perfectly prepared, and the beautiful dining room with its richly paneled walls lent a kind of magic to the whole evening. Melissa had trouble believing that she was sitting there in the company of a handsome and entertaining host who took all this elegance for granted. She hid a secret smile as she imagined him sitting at her marred Formica table on chairs that were losing their stuffing.

Once in a while she could hear Eric's and Richie's childish voices in the kitchen, and, although she missed them, she was grateful for the reprieve from their less-than-polished eating habits.

By the time they had finished their deep-dish apple pie and their after-dinner coffee, they had grown more comfortable in each other's presence. Once again the idea came to David to ask Melissa to be his companion for the fund-raiser. He knew she'd be a perfect companion for the evening. Undoubtedly it would be a different experience for her, with all the handshak-

ing and back-slapping, but she would charm them
with her lovely eyes and sweet smile. And if tonight
was any test, for a change he would finally enjoy
himself at one of these political affairs.

He wondered why he suddenly felt more self-
conscious asking her to go with him than he would
have approaching a formidable dignitary. "I would
like to ask a favor of you, Melissa."

Melissa waited, wondering why he suddenly
seemed ill at ease. This private time together had gone
well, hadn't it? Had she missed something? Was he
going to ask her and the boys to move out of the
house?

"Please, feel free to say no. There's an important
political fund-raiser next weekend. It's a reception,
banquet, and a national dinner speaker. I have to go."
He cleared his throat. "And I'm expected to take
someone with me. I was wondering—hoping, really,
that you might consider going as my dinner partner.
The food will be lousy, I can promise you that, but
you might find the political circus entertaining."

She had to smile at his not very persuasive presen-
tation. "It sounds interesting, but I wouldn't be comfortable at that kind of thing. Sorry."

"As a writer, I would have thought you'd be open
to new experiences." Her flat refusal didn't surprise
him but he wasn't about to accept it without an argument.

"My life is already full of new experiences," she
countered. Sitting here in this elegant dining room
with him was one of them. She pretended interest in
her coffee as she took another sip. She knew it wasn't

the challenge of spending an evening with Denver's rich and influential that was making her say no. It was the idea of going out with the esteemed David Ardell as his date that brought an instant refusal. He moved in elite social circles. The society pages were filled with the kind of women and social events that were a part of his life. She didn't belong in that kind of society whirl, now or ever.

"Thank you for the invitation." She shook her head. "I'm sorry."

"I'm sorry, too." He could tell from the finality in her tone that further discussion was pointless. "All right, then, I guess we'd better move on to the problem at hand. The dog."

She met his eyes. "Yes, let's talk about the dog. I want to explain what happened."

He leaned back in his chair. "Please do. Never in my life have I seen a more disreputable creature. It is really beyond me why you would allow the boys to have anything to do with it."

"I really didn't have much choice. The boys were playing in the backyard, and I was keeping an eye on them through the window. Inga set out a plate of sandwiches and some drinks on the patio table, and I intended to join them as soon as I finished what I was working on. The next time I looked out, I saw Eric and Richie on the grass with this dog, feeding him their sandwiches." She drew in a deep breath. "Apparently he came to the gate, whined and wanted in. You can guess the rest. The poor thing was starved."

"Why not feed him and then call Animal Control?"

"How could I? Before I knew it, the boys were pouring love on the stray as if they'd found something to make their lives less bleak. I told them the dog was the scruffiest-looking thing I'd ever seen, and they started calling him Scruffy. I think they identify with him because they've been hungry and alone. I just couldn't take the dog away from them."

"Well, I can," David said firmly. He'd never had a dog. Never wanted one. His mother had said they were nothing but nuisances and he agreed. "No dogs."

"We could keep him in the backyard and utility room. With a bath and trim, he might even look presentable," she argued.

"Be sensible about this, Melissa," he said as gently as his irritation would allow. "We've got two children to place, and so far, the investigator hasn't come up with any relative who might take them. As long as the children are here, there'll be no dog."

She looked at him with a stubborn set to her chin. "Let's make a deal. I'll go with you to the fund-raiser if you'll let the boys keep the dog."

He wanted to laugh. The idea that he would even be open to such an absurd bargain was ridiculous, and he couldn't believe that he didn't flatly reject the offer. "What kind of a deal is that?"

"A good one, don't you think? You get what you want, and the boys get what they want."

"And what do you get?" he asked with a teasing smile.

She grinned. "A chance to wear the new dress I just bought."

As his gaze swept over her animated, smiling face, he knew that, dog or no dog, he wasn't about to turn down the trade she'd offered. "It's a deal. Shall we shake on it?"

"Is that how you lawyers seal important deals like this one?" she asked.

"Absolutely." As she slipped her hand in his, he was tempted to let his fingers lightly stroke her soft smooth skin but he knew better. She wasn't the kind to engage in any casual dalliance, and he wasn't going to jeopardize the chance to spend an evening with Melissa instead of some boring debutante.

He couldn't quite figure out why she intrigued him so much, but he suspected that once the boys were placed, there was little chance their paths would cross again.

Chapter Four

The next morning when Melissa and the boys went down for breakfast, the dog was gone.

"Gone?" Melissa said in disbelief when Scruffy was nowhere to be seen. The boys began to wail loudly.

"You lied!" Eric clenched his little fists. "You said we could keep him."

Richie's dark eyes suddenly filled with tears. "I liked Scruffy. He was a neat dog. Why did you let someone take him away?"

"I'm sure there must be some mistake," Melissa soothed, trying to keep her own anger under control. She'd heard David's car leave early, so he must have decided to dispose of the dog before the boys got up. He'd skipped out of the house before the ax could fall. She couldn't believe that he'd gone back on the deal they'd made. Apparently he'd decided her company at the fund-raiser wasn't worth the hassle of putting up with a scrawny mutt for a few days.

Inga came into the breakfast room with a puzzled look on her face. "What's all the fuss about?"

Melissa tried to keep her voice even. Nothing would be gained by lighting into the housekeeper. "What did David do with the dog, Inga?"

"Oh, he told Hans to take him to some dog place."

"The dog pound?" Melissa asked, almost choking on the words.

"No, not the pound. You know, one of those place where they give dogs baths and trim them up nice. Hans was supposed to take the dog to the vet for some shots, too."

As a surge of relief swept over Melissa, she was surprised at her own quick reaction to think the worst. In fact, she was a little ashamed. David had been more than gracious to put up with this invasion of his home and privacy, and he had every right to protest keeping the dog. Melissa felt guilty about the way she had judged him, when, instead, he was spending money on the dog for grooming and shots. She was as bad as the boys.

"What happened to Scruffy?" Eric demanded, not understanding Inga's explanation and looking as worried as ever.

"It's all right, boys," Melissa assured them. She explained where Hans had taken the dog and why. She joked that they might have to change Scruffy's name to fit his new looks. "David just wanted to make sure the dog was all nice and clean and healthy."

"He must like Scruffy," Eric said, suddenly happy, his lips curving in a soft smile.

"David's a good guy," Richie agreed, in an instant change of heart.

Inga just shook her head. "Wonders never cease. A dog in the house. Heaven help us. I don't know what's gotten into David to allow it." Her clear eyes held a knowing glint as she looked at Melissa and added, "And then again, maybe I do."

The way the housekeeper was looking at her made Melissa stiffen. Surely the housekeeper didn't think that there was anything personal in allowing the boys to keep the dog. While she was trying to decide how to respond, Inga gave a teasing laugh.

"David spoke to me about keeping the boys on Friday night while you two go out," she said. "He wants his tux put in order and his silver cuff links polished. My, my, such a to-do." Inga's eyes held a merry sparkle as she asked solemnly, "Will you be needing my help getting ready for the special occasion? Your dating the governor's counselor will raise a few eyebrows."

All of a sudden Melissa wondered what she'd let herself in for by agreeing to accompany David to this political affair. She'd be on display as his companion. What in the world had she been thinking of? Maybe she should back out now before she embarrassed them both.

"It's really not a date," she corrected the housekeeper.

"Of course not," Inga agreed much too readily to be sincere. "David explained that you were just helping him out. He's always getting pressured to take someone—many times a woman he doesn't know—

to these affairs. It's nice that you're willing to go along with him.''

Melissa sighed. ''I don't know if he'll think so when I get all tongue-tied with some of his fancy friends, or say the wrong thing. Reading the society page is as close as I've ever gotten to this kind of shindig.''

''David wouldn't be taking you if he had any doubts about you. Just keep your head high and show them that pretty smile of yours, ya?''

''Ya,'' Melissa agreed with a chuckle.

Hans came back with the dog, who was all bathed and clipped. Scruffy still looked like a skinny, long-haired mutt, but the boys thought he was absolutely handsome. Now that Scruffy had had a bath, his coat was more caramel-colored than dirty brown. He couldn't have been more than two years old, and looked as if he might grow another head taller. His mixed heritage gave him long legs, a stubby body and long ears, but his friendliness made up for his un-gainly appearance.

As the boys tumbled in the grass with him, Melissa prayed that a family could be found for the boys that would also include an affectionate young dog. Every time she started to worry about what was going to happen to Richie and Eric if a relative couldn't be found to take them, she reminded herself, *Let go and let God.*

Melissa made a quick trip back to her apartment while the boys were down for their naps. She needed other things that she hadn't brought with her the first time. Certainly, attending a fancy function hadn't been in her thoughts when she packed her clothes for a few days' stay at the Ardell home.

With some misgivings, she drew her new summer dress from the closet. Somehow, it didn't look as chic as Melissa had remembered. At least she had two pieces of her grandmother's jewelry to wear with the lilac, floor-length dress. The amethyst necklace and earrings were as lovely as any offered in the modern stores. She touched them lovingly and murmured, "Granny, I'm going out on the town."

Go get 'em, girl.

Melissa could almost hear her beloved grandmother's voice as clearly as her own breath. Even after her death, the loving woman who had raised her never seemed far away, and her strength of faith and her courage were still guiding forces in Melissa's life. She knew that her grandmother would approve of the steps she'd taken to find a home for Eric and Richie. And even though her grandmother might not totally approve of David Ardell and his worldly lifestyle, Melissa knew that she would have applauded his willingness to suffer the presence of two playful children and an energetic dog in his home.

"What's this I hear about you making reservations for two at the fund-raiser?" Stella asked, breezing into David's office with a smile on her face. "Don't tell me you broke down and invited some lucky lady to go with you?"

"I don't know whether *lucky* is the right word," David countered, amused at Stella's open curiosity.

"But yes, I've invited someone to attend the affair with me," he admitted, and then purposefully let his eyes drop back to the paper he held in his hand, as if the subject was closed.

"Well, who is she?" Stella demanded, not the least bit put-off by his dismissive manner. "Did you finally ask Senator Wainwright's daughter? It's plain to anyone with eyes in his head that Pamela's been giving you the green light every time you're in the same room together. She's the perfect one for—"

"It's not Pamela Wainwright." David cut off her monologue of the attractive young woman's virtues. He was well aware that everyone, including the governor, had decided that Pamela Wainwright would be good for his political future. Her father had been in state politics for years, and Pamela was at ease in the fast-paced climate of elections and candidates. But David had found her company rather tiring and shallow. He'd avoided spending any more time with her than was necessary, and had resisted pressure to make them a twosome.

Stella raised an eyebrow. "Who, then? Do I sense some reluctance in your choice?"

"Not at all." David met her eyes directly. "I'm very pleased that she has consented to go with me."

"Well, do I know her?" Impatiently, Stella settled her hands on her hips. "Really, David, I don't understand what's going on here. Are you planning on making a grand entrance with some famous supporter on your arm? Is some movie star coming that I don't know about?" Her eyes sparkled. "That would be just like you—waltzing in with Hollywood's latest diva."

David silently groaned. He should have been open about taking Melissa and avoided all this unnecessary speculation. Now he would have to bring Stella up-to-date on the arrangement he'd made to keep two little boys and their temporary nanny.

"Have a seat, Stella," he said reluctantly. "I have some personal business that I suppose you ought to know about."

She listened without interruption as he explained how he had become responsible for finding a home for Jolene McCombre's two children. "The boys are staying at my house in the care of a young woman, Melissa Chanley, while an investigator searches for a relative to take them in. I talked with him this morning. Unfortunately, so far he's come up empty searching for relatives on the mother's side, but he is hopeful that something positive will break on the father's side."

"And what if it doesn't?" Stella asked bluntly. "Really, David, I think you've let yourself be drawn into a situation that's exploiting your good intentions. This Melissa Chanley sounds manipulative to me."

"Really? Well, I guess you'll have a chance to decide for yourself. She's the one I'm bringing to the fund-raiser."

Stella lost her voice for a moment and then sputtered, "You...you have to be kidding. How did this woman manage to get you to agree to such a thing?"

"You wouldn't believe it if I told you," David said, laughing.

"Don't you know how important it is for you to be seen with the right people, David? What is everyone going to think when you walk in with this woman?"

"They'll probably think that she's the most poised and beautiful woman in the room. Trust me, Stella, I won't have to make any apologies for Melissa Chanley, but I'm not sure how the rest of the company will measure up in her eyes." He frowned. "I don't think all the superficial folderol will impress her in the least."

Stella rose. "Let's just hope she doesn't make the kind of fool of herself that hits the papers."

Even though Melissa had covered some of Denver's social events when she was just out of college with her journalist degree and working briefly for one of the local newspapers, she'd never been a guest at any of the governor's affairs. Not in her most fanciful dreams had she pictured herself walking into a sparkling banquet hall with an escort as polished and suave as David Ardell.

As Melissa dressed for the important evening, she was filled with misgivings, and her hands trembled as she applied light makeup. What if she made some terrible faux pas? She couldn't bear to think that she might embarrass David in some way. When she was ready, she was almost afraid to go downstairs.

The boys were in the Erickson's apartment, playing a game with Hans while Inga was preparing dinner. Inga had promised to get them to bed early, and Melissa hoped they wouldn't give her a bad time before settling down.

As she walked down the stairs and across the foyer to the front parlor where he was surely waiting, she hoped he wouldn't be able to tell how rapidly her heart was beating. This was worse than going on a first date, she thought, but she put a smile on her lips and went on.

At the sound of her high heels on the marble floor, David turned and watched her move gracefully across the room. The soft folds of her dress fell in graceful swirls about her lithe figure. A necklace of small amethyst stone circled her neck, and matching earrings highlighted the smoothness of her lovely face and the upward sweep of shiny dark hair in a coil upon her head. As his eyes took in her loveliness, an undefined rush of emotion made him speechless.

"Is something the matter?" she asked anxiously, uncertain why his eyes were fixed so widely on her.

He was impeccably dressed in evening clothes, and had the air of someone who could wear a tuxedo, black tie and ruffled white shirt with the same ease that most fellows wear faded jeans and sweats. She despaired that she had been presumptuous enough to think she could fit into his high-class life, if only for one evening.

"Do I look all right?" she asked anxiously.

His dark eyes softened. "You look lovely, Melissa. Stunning, in fact."

"Are you sure? I mean, I'll understand if you want to change your mind. It might be better all around if—"

"Oh, no, you don't." He shook his head. "You're not going to back out now. We have a deal, remember? I can't promise you the most exciting evening in your life, but I'll do my best to keep you from being bored."

"Bored?" She laughed. "I doubt that very much."

"Good." Smiling, he made a mock bow. "Well, then, Ms. Chanley, shall we go have dinner with the governor and a few hundred others?"

"I'd be delighted," she said in the same playful tone.

Suppressed excitement radiating from her youthful spirit was infectious, and he found himself really looking forward to spending the evening with her. In the past two years, he'd attended so many state dinners, political rallies and fancy receptions that these affairs were now something to be endured—but not tonight. Her presence would cast a glow over the tedious proceedings.

They drove up to the posh hotel's entrance in David's deluxe black sedan, and a young valet in a smart uniform instantly hurried forward to greet them. Melissa suppressed a smile, wondering how the officious valet would react if he had to park her ten-year-old, secondhand car with its uncertain paint job.

Once inside the glittering lobby, Melissa was grateful for David's guiding hand as he led her to an elevator. They emerged on the second floor, where a cluster of fashionably attired men and women were already filing into a huge banquet hall.

David began nodding and smiling, but Melissa sensed there was little warmth in the exchange of po-

lite greetings. She felt questioning eyes upon her, but
no one gave her more than a polite nod, until an attractive gray-haired woman in a silver lamé gown approached them.

"David, I believe you and your guest are at my
table," she said with a bright smile, and as her sharp
eyes locked on Melissa's face, she held out a long,
slender hand. "Stella Day. I'm pleased to meet you,
Ms. Chanley."

"Thank you, my pleasure," Melissa responded,
wondering if the attractive woman knew more about
her than just her name. The way Ms. Day's sharp eyes
were traveling over her gave Melissa the impression
that the woman was more than just casually interested
in her. How much had David told Ms. Day about the
boys? Was she aware of the fact that he was bringing
a "nanny" to this gala event?

"Stella is an executive assistant to the governor,"
David explained. "She keeps us all in line."

She gave a self-depreciating wave of her hand. "I
just try to guide David as best I can, but I'm not
always successful." Stella smiled at him, her tone
clearly indicating that this might be one of those
times.

"You must have a fascinating and rewarding job."
Melissa smiled, steadily meeting the woman's eyes.
"I can't even imagine the challenges that go with that
kind of responsibility. It must be overwhelming sometimes."

"Yes, it is," Stella answered, her expression softening.

David suppressed a grin. Good girl, Melissa, he

thought. A flattering interest worked every time, even with a seasoned veteran like Stella.

"If you'll follow me, I'll show you to our table," Stella said. "I checked the place cards earlier."

"And moved them around to your satisfaction?" David chided, skeptical that they had ended up at the same table by chance.

"You could say that," she admitted with a smile.

Melissa was grateful for David's hand in hers as they followed Stella to the front of the banquet hall near the speaker's platform. Melissa was nervous, and David must have felt the sweat beading on her palm, because he squeezed her hand and whispered, "You're the most charming woman here. Relax and enjoy yourself."

"I'll try," she said, but she wondered how she could do credit to the five-hundred-dollar-a-plate dinner. Magnificent chandeliers hung from a high ceiling, and individual candles were placed on the tables along with the flowers, sparkling crystal goblets and silver tableware.

When they met several state congressmen and their wives, who were also taking their places at various tables, David hastened to introduce Melissa. He was delighted at the ease with which she handled the barrage of names.

As Stella led them to a round table with eight other people, David silently fumed. Two of them were Senator Wainwright and his daughter, Pamela. He knew that the seating was a deliberate ploy on Stella's part. She avoided looking at him as she quickly sat down at her place.

David introduced Melissa to the other dinner guests, and she was well aware of the curious exchange of glances among them. Obviously they were wondering who she was, and there was particular interest from a very attractive blonde seated directly across from David. The blonde was introduced as Pamela Wainwright, the senator's daughter, and Melissa's own curiosity was aroused when she intercepted a questioning look the young woman sent David. She couldn't help but wonder if David had been expected to take the woman to this affair. Had they been dating?

All during the meal, he seemed to pointedly ignore Pamela, even when Stella tried to draw the two of them into a conversation about a mutual friend. Most of the table conversation revolved around people and issues that had little meaning for Melissa. When personal questions were directed to her, she answered them honestly, explaining that she was a freelance writer and doing research for a book.

The fact that she could hold her own in a company that was alien to her background impressed David. He was enjoying the evening's political hype more than he had expected. Since he had been brought up with the never-ending political speeches and party "hurrah," he couldn't imagine a different kind of life for himself. As the evening ended, he hoped that maybe, just maybe, he might persuade Melissa to accompany him again to one of these affairs.

On the ride home, he noticed that her earlier bubbling eagerness had given way to quiet contemplation. "Tired?" he asked.

She nodded. "A little."

"I'm sorry the speeches were so long. I've never met a politician yet who ran out of words before he put his audience to sleep. What did you think of the governor?"

"He seems very energetic and popular. Quite a shrewd politician, I gather." She glanced at David's handsome profile. "Stella told me in confidence that he's grooming you for big things." Melissa didn't add that Stella had added that David couldn't afford to offend people like Senator Wainwright.

David wondered what else Melissa had heard about the party's plans for his political future. "I was hoping we might go somewhere and talk for a little while."

She shook her head. "I don't think so. I'm ready to call it a night." Even though she had enjoyed being with David, the superficial, charged atmosphere of the evening was not to her liking. Her values were too different from those of the people she'd met that evening who were playing roles and trying to impress guests they thought were more important. She firmly believed that individual worth came from within, and not from the opinions held by others in this competitive, often unloving world.

"Does this mean you're tired of my company?" he challenged. "I really was hoping that we might do this again sometime."

She ignored the question in his voice. The evening had been an interesting experience, but her glimpse into his social life made it clear that he'd been brought up in a lifestyle that was completely foreign to her. In truth, she felt as if she'd lost something important by going out with him. It would have been better to confine their contact to the house and the boys' welfare. She had no desire to hear any more about his political ambitions.

"I think I'd better be checking on the boys. They could have turned your house upside down by now," she said lightly.

He got her message loud and clear. She was going to keep their relationship on an impersonal level. "I'm sure Inga was able to handle them."

"I really appreciate your patience with them. Hopefully, we'll be out of your hair before long." She asked him about Mr. Weiss's search, and he brought her up-to-date on the investigator's progress, or lack of it.

"If he reaches a dead end trying to locate a relative, we'll have to look at other options," he warned her.

She knew what he meant, but she wasn't about to consider the idea that Eric and Richie would have to be turned over to foster parents. Stubbornly she held to her faith that they would find the right home and loving care for them.

"Everything is moving in divine order," she said with a stubborn lift to her chin. "We just have to be patient. If you feel that you no longer want to continue with our arrangement, I'll try to find some other accommodations for the boys and me."

His temper flared. "I wasn't asking you to move out. You're welcome to stay as long as is necessary, but I think you need to be realistic about this situation."

"I am realistic." She smiled at him sweetly. "Just look how nicely things have gone so far. The boys have a nice place to stay, and now they even have a dog."

He couldn't help but laugh. "You're point is made."

After they parked the car and quietly slipped into the house, Melissa thanked him again for the evening. He just nodded and said, "Thank you for going with me."

She quickly turned away, leaving him in the kitchen as she raced upstairs.

She was hurrying through her bedroom to check on the boys in the adjoining room, when she saw a little figure sleeping in the middle of her bed.

She thought it was Richie who had taken advantage of the situation to try out her queen-size bed, and she smiled, but as she came closer, she saw Eric curled up and hugging one of the soft pillows. Unbidden tears came to her eyes as she looked down at his tender, innocent face. There must be a loving home waiting for him and Richie somewhere.

Some inner voice chided her for running away from David earlier. Was she afraid to spend a few minutes of quiet time with him? Was she afraid that she'd lose her perspective? The answer to both questions seemed to be yes.

Chapter Five

When Melissa and the boys came down to breakfast on Sunday, all dressed for church, they found David getting ready to go play golf.

"I'll probably eat at the club," he told Inga. "We've got a foursome set up for eighteen holes. The governor wants me to see if I can smooth out some rough spots in a new bill these fellows are proposing."

"Business, always business. Better you be going to church."

David smiled. "I've told you before, Inga, I'm putting my church-going in your name."

Inga turned to Melissa. "I give up. The only time he sees the inside of a church is when someone is buried or married."

"You're welcome to come with me and the boys," Melissa invited, knowing before he shook his head that he was going to refuse. Keeping the sabbath holy was not on David Ardell's agenda.

Melissa took the boys with her to a small church that she and her grandmother had attended. Located on the western edge of the city in the shadow of the nearby Rocky Mountains, the tranquil setting always made the sabbath especially renewing for her. Melissa had taken Eric and Richie twice before while they were in her care, and the small congregation had warmly welcomed them.

"They're bright little boys," the Sunday School teacher told Melissa. "Eric doesn't say much, but Richie takes it all in and isn't shy about telling you what he thinks."

Melissa nodded in agreement. She never knew what Richie was going to say. When a kind, elderly lady fussed over the boys, saying sadly, "I'm so sorry that you've lost your mother," Richie spoke up with indignation, "My mama's not lost. She's in heaven."

Melissa hid a smile and thanked the lady for her concern. She felt the support of the church family, and an elderly minister assured her that the children's names were on the prayer list and reminded her, "Trust in the Lord, and he will direct your paths."

On Monday morning that assurance seemed to be fulfilled when David called from his office and told Melissa that he was bringing Sidney Weiss home for lunch. "Will you ask Inga to prepare something simple, and we'll eat on the patio? I have to be back to the office for another appointment at two."

"Does the investigator have some good news?" Melissa asked anxiously, her heart suddenly beating in double time.

"I'm not sure. Don't get your hopes up too high,"

he warned. "Sidney will explain everything at lunch."

The morning crept by with agonizing slowness. Melissa couldn't keep her mind on work, and the boys seemed to be especially trying, fussing over the same swing, or arguing about whose turn it was on the jungle gym. Inga was irritable about the unexpected guest for lunch, so Melissa volunteered to make some sandwiches for the boys and feed them early. She had them settled down with coloring books in the sitting room, when David and the investigator arrived.

Sidney Weiss was a small, full-faced man with smiling eyes behind brown-rimmed glasses. He was somewhere in his late forties, and Melissa liked him at once. She tried to control her impatience to know why David had brought him home, but as they took their places around the glass-topped table on the patio, Melissa realized that nothing was going to be said to enlighten her about his visit until after they had enjoyed the seafood salad and fruit cobbler that Inga had prepared.

She forced herself to smile and contribute to the general conversation as if there was nothing on her mind but being an entertaining hostess, but an exciting quivering in her stomach affected her appetite. She was relieved when Inga served coffee and David leaned forward in his chair, signaling that the time for business had arrived.

"We appreciate your taking the time to personally bring us up-to-date in your investigation. I thought Melissa should hear directly what you have to say."

"My pleasure." Sidney reached into his jacket

pocket and brought out a small notebook. "I'm sorry that even after using our considerable resources for tracking down people, I failed to find close members of the McCombre family who might be suitable to adopt two small boys. As you know—" he nodded at David "—Jolene was an only child of middle-aged parents who passed away several years ago. We found two of her cousins, but unfortunately one of them is engulfed in an ugly divorce and the other has extreme financial problems. I can provide you with their names and addresses."

"The children need a stable, secure environment," Melissa said quickly. "They've already suffered too much upheaval in their young lives."

"What about the father's family?" David asked briskly. "Any better luck?"

"A little." Sidney's expression brightened slightly as he flipped a page in his notebook. "We located an aunt of the boy's father. Her name is Paula Bateman. She is single, never married, and is in her late forties."

Melissa's heart fell. "I'm not sure that she'd want to tackle the raising of two small boys at her age."

"What about her finances?" David asked, cutting to the essentials as he saw them.

Sidney checked his notes. "She's financially independent from the sale of land that was homesteaded by her grandparents. Our reports indicate that Paula Bateman is a very respected member of the small community of Wolfton, Montana." He handed David a piece of paper. "This is her address and telephone number."

"Well, what do you think, Melissa?" David asked, searching her face.

She couldn't bring herself to answer. She'd been praying for a young couple to take the boys, not a middle-aged, single woman. Surely, this wasn't the answer for Eric and Richie. "Are you sure there's no one else?"

"I'm afraid not. We've investigated comprehensive family trees on both the mother's and father's sides, and Paula Bateman is the only relative in the picture who could possibly offer to take them in."

David watched Melissa's crestfallen expression replace the hopeful eagerness that had been there a moment before. "It wouldn't hurt to give her a call, Melissa."

"I suppose not," she agreed reluctantly.

David knew she had expected Sidney to come up with the perfect solution to their problem, but this aunt might be the boys' only hope.

"I think you should call her," Sidney said. "After talking with her, you may have a better feel for whether putting the boys in her care would be feasible. After all, she may flatly refuse to have anything to do with them—and that will be that."

David agreed. He knew Melissa was dead set against any foster care, and he didn't like the idea much either—if they had another choice.

"I'm sorry," the investigator said, preparing to leave. "I wanted to explore every possibility before completing my report. Of course, you're free to hire someone else, but I'm confident that we have turned over every bit of ground in our search."

David shook hands with him and thanked him for his services. After he'd gone, David turned to Melissa and asked gently, "Do you want to make the call, or shall I?"

She was tempted to say, *You do it,* but she took a deep breath and replied, "Maybe I'd better talk with her, but I'm not sure I'll be able to tell much about her on the phone."

"Just explain the situation and see how she reacts." He gave her a wry grin as he teased, "You're good at that. Remember how deftly you dumped all of this in my lap?"

She smiled back at him, and as their eyes held, an unbidden sense of intimacy sparked between them. Even though he made no move to touch her, she felt a tender caress in his eyes. She looked away quickly, trying to ignore a sudden warmth that eased into her cheeks.

"I want to think about what I'm going to say before I call her."

"I bet you're as persuasive over the phone as you are in person," he encouraged.

"But what if this isn't the right home for Eric and Richie?"

"But what if it is?"

"I guess there's only one way to find out." She looked at the paper that had Paula's number on it. "Do you want to listen in on the call?"

He glanced at his watch. "No, I've got to rush. I'll be in conference all afternoon but I'll try to get home early enough tonight so you can fill me in." He gave her shoulder a light squeeze as they walked into the house. "Good luck."

Melissa waited until the boys were down for a nap before she sat down at her desk and dialed the number the investigator had given her. She cleared her voice several times as the phone was ringing, and was about to conclude that no one was home, when the receiver was picked up.

"Hello." The woman sounded a little out of breath.

"Paula Bateman?"

"That's me. Look, will you hold a minute? I ran in from outside and didn't get the screen door shut tight. Those pesky squirrels will follow me in to see what's in my cupboard if I let them." She gave a short laugh, followed by a clatter of the receiver and the muffled sound of a door slamming. "There, that's better. Sorry to keep you waiting."

"That's all right," Melissa assured her, caught off-guard by the woman's breezy manner, which made her own rehearsed speech seem much too stiff and formal. "My grandmother had a couple of squirrels that were determined to make a home in the porch roof. We finally gave up and let them raise three litters there."

"Just be glad they weren't skunks." Paula laughed, a nice full, robust laugh, and Melissa's spirits began to rise.

"Ms. Bateman, I—"

"It's Paula. We use first names around here."

"I'm Melissa Chanley, calling from Denver," Melissa explained. "Your name was given to me as

Edward McCombre's aunt." She tried to keep her voice light and friendly. "Do I have the right party?"

"Land sakes, Eddie was my nephew, all right. There were never any close ties between us, but when I heard about his dying young like that, it was sad."

"Did you know his wife, Jolene?"

"Never met her. Last I heard, he left her with a couple of babies."

"Well, those babies are now wonderful little boys, four and six years old. Their names are Eric and Richie. I'm sorry to tell you that their mother, Jolene, recently passed away." She waited until Paula had made sympathetic sounds and then added, "I'm a friend who is looking after the boys until we can find a permanent home for them. And that's why I'm calling you. We want very much to place Eric and Richie with a relative who will love and care for them."

"Oh, I sure hope you find someone, but I can't think of anyone on Eddie's side of the family who could take the youngsters and raise them."

"What about…you?"

Paula's answer was booming laughter so loud that Melissa had to hold the receiver away from her. "Me, raising two young'uns, that's a hoot!" she bellowed. "Now, if you were talking about an abandoned colt or an orphaned fawn, that would be something different, but I don't know nothing about raising kids."

"They just need the same kind of love as any of God's creatures," Melissa offered. "And they're very good teachers, believe me."

"Land sakes, I'm on the downside of forty. Too old to be saddling myself with that kind of responsibility. There's no way on God's green earth that I would agree to take on Eddie's kids.''

Melissa swallowed back her disappointment. ''Won't you take some time to think about it?''

''It turned out that the good Lord didn't see fit to give me a family of my own, and it's too late in life for me to be raising someone else's kids.''

There was such finality in her voice that Melissa didn't know what else she could say. ''I understand. Thank you for being honest.'' If the aunt didn't want the boys, they didn't belong with her.

''I wouldn't mind seeing the little fellows.'' Paula softened her tone. ''For a visit, that is. Nothing more. Of course, if you've got someone else to take them right away…?''

''No, we haven't,'' Melissa answered as evenly as her disappointment would allow. ''Our plans for the boys are up in the air.''

''Good, then why don't you bring them around for a nice visit? My house is a big old thing, built by my parents on the side of a mountain. Real pretty country, too. Ever been to Montana?''

''No, but I don't think it's feasible to take the boys on a trip right now.''

''Too bad. I'd really like to see Eddie's kids sometime.''

''I'll pass the word along to whomever takes the boys,'' Melissa promised, trying to keep her voice positive.

Well, that's that, she thought after she thanked the aunt and hung up.

* * *

When David came home that evening, the boys had already gone to bed and Melissa was working at her computer in the sitting room. From the half-hearted smile that Melissa gave him, he suspected that the telephone call to Paula Bateman had not gone well.

"Long day?" she asked, as he dropped down onto a comfortable floral sofa and stretched his long legs out in front of him.

He nodded. "How about you?"

"Longer than usual." She faced him, clasping her hands on the desk and meeting his questioning eyes. "Paula Bateman won't take the boys."

"I can't say that I'm surprised," he admitted. "It was a long shot at best."

"I know, but she's the only lead we have. The sad thing is, I think she'd be good with them." Melissa repeated the telephone conversation as best she could. "Obviously she has a good heart. She said she'd love to have the boys come for a visit but adamantly refused to consider taking them permanently."

"She said they could come for a visit?" He perked up.

"Yes, but I told her that it wasn't possible because everything is too unsettled."

David frowned thoughtfully. "Maybe a visit is not a bad idea."

"Are you serious?"

"Sure, why not? Let her get acquainted with Eric and Richie. There's a chance she might get hooked and want to keep them. Of course, there's just as good a chance that she'll be happy to send them on their

way," he added wryly, "but it's worth a try, don't
you agree?"

She just stared at him. "You think I should take
the boys all the way to Montana to visit an aunt who
doesn't want them?" There was a dull ache in her
chest. Was David so anxious to have them out of his
house that he was willing to bet on the long shot that
the aunt would change her mind and absolve him of
any more responsibility?

"You said she invited them for a visit. Why not
accept and see how things go?"

"And just how would we get there?" Melissa said
tersely. "Drive my vintage car?" She was lucky to
make it across town without something breaking
down.

"You're not afraid of flying, are you? I could look
into some possible flights to Wolfton, Montana, if you
decide to go."

"It seems to me that you've already decided," she
said, more sharply than she had intended.

Her barb had hit its mark. His mouth tightened.
"No, I haven't decided anything. I'm just going on
what you've said—that Paula Bateman might change
her mind if she had the chance to know the boys. It's
your decision, Melissa. I'll finance the trip and make
the arrangements, if you want me to."

"Let me think about it."

He didn't know what else to say. Turning the boys
over to a state agency was not to his liking, either,
but Sidney's exhaustive search had not turned up any
other relative. Paula Bateman was their only hope for
placing the boys with family.

"I'm sorry if I've upset you, Melissa. I just feel that if there's a chance that Paula might change her mind, we ought to take it—don't you?"

Melissa got up from her chair and walked over to the window. She stared at the purple night sky, weighing David's suggestion. She had to admit that there was some merit in letting Paula get acquainted with the boys. Even if their great-aunt couldn't take them permanently, she would be aware of their existence, and that could work to their advantage whatever happened.

"I'm only trying to figure out the best course to take," David said, defending himself. He knew that he'd cast himself in a bad light. "I wasn't trying to get rid of you by suggesting that you take the boys to visit their aunt. I just think saying no over the phone is a lot easier than doing it in person."

He was surprised when she walked over to the small sofa and sat down beside him. Her nearness made him aware of her appealing femininity. Her pink knit top and soft white slacks nicely molded to her slender figure, and her dark hair was pulled back by a pink ribbon into a ponytail. As he felt the sweet length of her warm body sitting so close to his, he boldly let one arm rest casually behind her shoulders as she talked.

"I think you may be right," she admitted. "If Paula has a chance to know and love the boys, it could only be a plus in their lives. Taking them to visit her is a gamble, I know, and it's very generous of you to suggest the trip. You really don't have to do this. It's enough that you've turned your whole house over to us.''

"There are compensations," he said, enjoying the sudden closeness that they were sharing. She had relaxed against the curve of his arm, and he could feel a sudden excitement in her replacing the initial disappointment. At that moment, he wondered why he'd been such a fool as to suggest that she take off for Montana and leave him with an empty house echoing with loneliness.

She felt his arm tightening around her shoulder, and for a moment she didn't know what to do. The easy companionship they'd been experiencing was suddenly gone, and something deeper and more intimate was threatening to take its place. She knew that if she turned and looked at him, she would invite his kiss. Her feelings threatened to spin out of control, and it frightened her.

"I'll call Paula in the morning and make sure she meant the invitation," she said, easing to her feet. The timing was right for a change of scenery, she thought. And maybe none too soon.

He was already gone the next morning, when Melissa made the telephone call to Paula and accepted her invitation to bring the boys for a visit.

Melissa was too excited to wait until evening to tell David. Impulsively, she called his office. His secretary answered, about to run interference on his calls until Melissa said her name.

"Oh yes, Ms. Chanley," Elsie said so sweetly that

Melissa guessed the gossip about her ''date'' with David had made the rounds.

She had never called him before, and when he heard her voice, he asked anxiously, ''Is something wrong?''

''No, not at all. In fact, I have good news,'' she reassured him, and explained that she'd organized the visit with Paula. ''I thought you might want to start making plans.''

''I'll get right on it, and tell you tonight what I've arranged.'' He wanted to keep her on the line longer, but as usual he was pressed for time. Feeling that when he'd held her close last night he'd overstepped the bounds they'd set, he wasn't sure how to apologize. Certainly trying to say anything over the phone wasn't a good idea. ''I'll check and see what's the best way we can fly you and the boys to Wolfton, Montana.''

When he reported to her that evening, it turned out that there wasn't a best way. In fact, making airline connections to Wolfton proved nearly impossible. Wolfton was miles from any commercial airport. Only small puddle-jumper airplanes fly anywhere close to the town, and none of their schedules matched.

''You'd make better time driving instead of taking small hit-and-miss charter flights,'' David told Melissa, exasperated. ''You'll need a car once you get to that mountain town, anyway.''

''How long a drive is it?''

''You can make it in two days if you do some hard driving.'' As he saw the flicker of apprehension in her eyes, he added quickly, "Of course, you could spend two or three nights out if you decided to take it slow. You'll have to drive all across the state of Wyoming and into Montana. Think you can do it?"

"Of course I can do it." Her eyes snapped at the fact he'd dared to question her driving ability.

He chuckled at her feisty response. "Good. I've got some maps of Wyoming and Montana. We'll mark out the best route."

"Are you loaning us your car?" she asked boldly. If they weren't going to fly, they'd have to have something decent to drive.

"I'll see about a rental. Any car preference?"

"One big enough to hold two boys and a dog."

"You're taking the dog?" His eyes rounded in disbelief. "Are you out of your mind?"

"Probably, but I don't have a choice."

"Of course you do," he argued. "It's going to be a long drive at best. Why saddle yourself with the added stress of taking a dog?"

"Because the boys will have a fit if I leave Scruffy here. They love that dog too much to part with," she said frankly. "Besides, if our little plan works and the boys remain with Paula, I'll feel better about leaving them if they have the dog with them."

"Are you going to be all right driving back alone?"

She just smiled. "Don't worry, I'll bring the car and myself back in one piece."

He wasn't entirely comfortable with the idea of Melissa traveling by herself, but he knew better than to argue the point.

They spread the maps out on the desk, and almost immediately David realized that she wasn't going to take his suggestions about which route to take. She listened politely to what he had to say and then pointed out a different route that was a little longer, but would take them through one corner of Yellowstone National Park.

"You can't make any time going through Yellowstone," he said with macho authority.

"I know, but the boys would love seeing some of the wildlife and so would I. They say that deer and buffalo wander right down the highway." Her eyes sparkled. "And I've always wanted to see Old Faithful geyser. It seems a shame to go right by the park and not take a little time to see some of it."

"If you go that way, you'll lose half a day's traveling."

"Or gain half a day's pleasure? It depends on how you look at it, doesn't it?"

He gave up. Obviously she wasn't going to follow his advice about making the trip as speedily as possible. If she wanted to dally with two kids and an overgrown dog, the choice was hers. He'd make sure she had enough travelers' checks to take care of expenses, and that was the end of his responsibility. Wasn't it? She'd never made the slightest suggestion that he might go with them, and even if he wanted to, his commitments made it virtually impossible to drop everything and leave town.

When Melissa saw his frown and the weary lines around his mouth, she said with her usual candor,

"You look tired. Maybe things will be easier for you with us gone."

"Easier?" he echoed. "That isn't the word I would have chosen." He was going to miss the brief contacts he had had with her while she'd been in the house. When he came home late and tired, the place was no longer empty, and there was a different feel to it. Even scattered toys were somehow reassuring. He knew that she was critical of his lifestyle and lack of spiritual convictions, but he regretted that she was ready and eager to put an end to the arrangement they'd made for the boys. "You're welcome to stay as long as necessary."

"That's generous of you, but you don't need us around to complicate your life. If things don't work out with Paula, it's time to look for a different answer."

"And what would that be?"

"I don't know, but I'm certain Someone does. There's a divine pattern here, but we just can't see it."

He silently scoffed at her naive belief, but kept his skepticism to himself. If she wanted to delude herself that an answer was going to fall from the sky, it was her choice. He knew that hard facts about the children's future would have to be faced soon enough.

David tried to distance himself from preparations for the trip, but he was concerned about any unforeseen problems that might arise. He decided not to trust a rental car, but let her have his Lexus so he could quit being anxious about having the car break down in the middle of nowhere. How would he ever forgive himself if there was an accident?

He was *determined* not to get any more involved. So no one was more surprised than he was when what started as a nagging in his mind became, over the course of the next few days, a decision, full-blown and definite. The mountain of work remained. His tight schedule included appointments with important people like the Lieutenant Governor.

But one day he called his secretary into his office and said, "I'm going to be out of town for a few days. I have to make a trip to Montana."

Chapter Six

David had wanted to get an early start on the trip, but it was mid-morning before they finally got on the road. The boys were in the back with Scruffy, who was taking up most of the seat between them. While Melissa endeavored to keep them busy with quiet activities, David concentrated on making up as much time as the speed limit would allow. He finally began to relax when they left Colorado and crossed the Wyoming border, but his satisfaction was short-lived.

A few miles out of Cheyenne, Richie announced loudly, "I gotta go."

"Me, too," Eric added.

When Melissa saw David's jaw tighten, she asked, "I don't suppose we need gas or anything?"

"We've only covered a hundred miles," he answered shortly. He was used to getting behind the wheel and thinking about business as the hours went by. He couldn't believe that they were making a stop even before the trip really got started.

"There's a rest stop ahead," Melissa said. "It'll only take a quick minute."

Somehow the quick minute turned into more than fifteen. Scruffy had to be leashed and allowed to explore the dog run. He seemed more interested in bounding about than in anything else, and Melissa knew the energetic young dog wasn't going to take to hours of inactivity in the back seat of a car. Even though she had been delighted when David decided to drive them, she wondered now if it had been a good idea. Obviously the "stop and go" of his young passengers was not his idea of travel.

She had to give him credit for trying to accommodate the needs of his young travelers. "I take it you've never been on a trip with youngsters before."

He shook his head. "I was an only child. When my family traveled, we held to a rigid timetable. In fact, we'd just get to our destination and my father would set an itinerary for leaving."

"Not much fun for a kid," she said. No wonder he wasn't very spontaneous.

"What now?" he asked in disbelief, when Melissa and the boys disappeared into a curio shop adjoining a gas station, while he waited impatiently outside with the dog. He kept glancing at his watch, wondering if he should have made arrangements to be gone for a fourteen-day trip instead of three.

"Look what we got," Richie said excitedly, drawing some plastic dinosaurs out of a sack. "Melissa said they used to live around here."

"I got cowboys," Eric said solemnly. "Wyoming's full of cowboys."

David swallowed back his impatience and forced a smile. "What? Nothing for Scruffy and me?"

"Would you like us to go back and see if we can find something?" Melissa asked with an amused glint in her eyes.

"Maybe at the next stop," he answered. "Ten minutes from now."

The Wyoming highway ran north through rolling hills of mustard-colored grass with unrelieved vistas in every direction. As they traveled across the open country, Melissa realized how sparse the population was and how far apart the towns were. She breathed a prayerful thanks that she wasn't out on this barren road alone with the boys. She had been utterly astounded when David told her he'd arranged to drive her. He told her that depending on what happened with Paula and the boys, he'd make arrangements for her to get back to Denver.

Melissa had called her editor to explain that she'd be out of town for a short time. She was totally surprised when the woman told her that an editor's job was going to open at another magazine. She asked if Melissa would be interested.

"Would I ever," Melissa had exclaimed. A steady salary instead of depending upon freelance articles would ease her tight budget considerably.

"Good. We'll talk about it when you get back."

Melissa wanted to tell David about the offer, but held back. Somehow she felt that her little milestone wouldn't impress anyone else very much, especially someone whose career goals were set as high as David's.

"How far are we going to go tonight?" she asked, as the sun slipped out of sight on the flat horizon.

"Not as far as I planned," he said reluctantly. There was no way they would make it to the town he had picked on the map to have dinner and spend the night. "Let's look for a place to stop in the next hour."

When they spied a rustic motel stretched along the Platte River, David decided to check it out.

"The cabins are small," he reported back. "You and the boys could have one, and I'll take the dog with me in the other one."

"What about dinner?"

"Well, that depends," he said, winking at her. "They have a small fishing pond set up for kids with trout swimming around in it. Do you suppose Eric and Richie might want to try catching our supper? The motel's got someone who'll cook the trout for us. How does that sound?"

An excited clamor in the back seat was his answer. Melissa was amazed at this spontaneous adjustment on his part to the situation. Maybe there was hope for him yet.

After they checked in, a lanky, soft-spoken fellow who owned the motel gave the boys fishing poles and a can of worms.

"Ugh," Eric said, looking at the slimy bait. Then he looked wistfully at David. "You show me how?"

Melissa secretly smiled when David ended up baiting both the hooks. With his trousers rumpled from kneeling on the ground and his hair hanging over his forehead, he didn't look like the governor's efficient counselor. The feeling that welled in her on seeing him in this new light created a peculiar tightening in her chest, warning that she was treading on dangerous ground. Because she had grown up alone with her grandmother, she had not experienced the joy and fullness of family life. More than any personal success, she wanted a husband, children and a marriage blessed with God's goodness. As she watched David with the boys, she knew that his interest was only temporary. He'd made it clear where his true commitment lay. There was no room in his life for anything but his driving ambition.

The fact that the hungry fish practically jumped out of the water to be caught didn't diminish the boys' excitement in landing four beautiful rainbow trout. They proudly handed them to the owner's wife, and were eagerly ready to eat them when she brought the meal out of the kitchen.

Eric wanted to take some of his fish to Scruffy, who'd been left in the cabin, but he was finally persuaded that the dry dog food they'd brought along was a better choice.

"Do you think there's any chance we could get an earlier start tomorrow?" David asked hopefully, as they were finishing a dessert of cherry cobbler and rich cream. "I'd like to drive into Wolfton before dark tomorrow, and if we spend any time in Yellowstone, it's going to be a push."

"How early is early?"

"Six o'clock," he said, hoping for seven.

"I'd best get these guys to bed, then."

He started to say something, but the insistent ring

of a cell phone in his jacket pocket stopped him. "Excuse me." He got up from the table and walked away to take the call.

As he stood in the doorway of the hall, Melissa watched his expression change. Whatever was being said deepened lines in his forehead and shifted his easy, relaxed posture into one of rigid tenseness. When he returned to the table, the governor's counselor was back.

"I'll see you and the boys to your cabin," he said briskly. "Something's come up that needs my attention."

"Tonight?"

He gave a brisk nod. "The governor has appointed me to an important committee with influential people who could be an asset to my future. I have to get some thoughts down on paper right away. Fortunately, I brought my laptop along, just in case."

"Maybe you shouldn't have come prepared to work," she said, disturbed by the power that one telephone call had over him. All signs of the boyish fisherman were gone, and she could tell that his mind was already back on business. It both saddened her and made her angry that he was willing to sacrifice all personal enjoyment for the sake of his political ambitions.

Where your treasure is, there will be your heart, also. She knew very well where David Ardell's heart lay. A few glimpses into a different side of him didn't change his basic nature. She knew he was anxious to get the trip over with so he could get back to Denver as soon as possible.

She had trouble sleeping, and was aware that the light in his cabin stayed on late into the night. As she turned restlessly in her bed, she tried to sort out the tangle of her own emotions where he was concerned. She'd never felt like this before. Several times she had dated rather seriously, but there never had been anyone to set her emotions on edge the way David did. If the boys' future had not been involved, she would have walked away from him in a minute. Obviously, he was not the man to give her the kind of spiritual life and Christian home that she desired. She wanted a soul mate. Someone to pray with her, attend church with her, and read God's word as a daily ritual. She wanted someone beside her who was strong enough in his own faith to meet the challenges of life. David Ardell was not that man. She knew that. She also knew that getting her feelings muddled over him would lead her down a path that would be disastrous for both of them.

The next morning after a fitful sleep, she awoke just as dawn was breaking. After quietly dressing, she sat on her bed, reading her Bible and spending time in meditation. The daily scripture was Ephesians 1:18. ''I pray that your hearts will be flooded with light so that you can see something of the future he had called you to share.'' She found reassurance in the promise that her future was in His hands, and that her heart would make the right decisions.

At six, she woke the boys and left them to finish dressing while she walked over to David's cabin. She knocked on his door with smug satisfaction that he couldn't complain about them oversleeping.

No one answered.

She wondered if he'd worked until early morning and was sleeping too soundly to hear the knocking. Better not disturb him. Scruffy would wake him up soon enough, she decided, and she started to turn away.

"Melissa."

She swung around and saw that David and Scruffy were a short distance away, heading toward the river. He waved for her to come along, and as she hurried toward them she suddenly felt wonderfully alive. The morning air was brisk. A brilliant orange sun was rising on the horizon and touching the hills with gold.

As she fell in step beside him, he said, "I thought we ought to let the hound have a run before we coop him up in the car again."

"How did you two get along?"

"He snores," David said, smiling. Tired lines around his eyes hinted at a sleepless night, but there was an energetic pace to his steps, as Scruffy bounded ahead of them.

She was surprised when he reached out and took her hand as they walked. He'd never made that kind of gesture before, and she didn't know quite what to do, but the sound of the river flowing smoothly over polished rocks and lapping gently against the bank was in harmony with an unexpected companionship between them.

"Are you a morning person?" he asked.

"I guess so." She chuckled. "My grandmother was always quoting, 'Early to bed, early to rise, makes a gal healthy, wealthy and wise.' It's a habit with me now.''

He had suddenly realized how little he knew about her, even though she seemed able to fill up the empty places in his life without any effort. After a few minutes of asking questions about her personal life, he saw color sweep up into her cheeks when he said bluntly, ''I don't understand why you're not married. I mean, you love children, that's obvious, and from the way the fellows at the fund-raiser were looking at you, I'd say you could attract about any man you wanted.''

''I guess that's your answer.'' She lightly tossed her head. ''I haven't found one that I wanted.''

''That picky, huh?'' His grin teased her.

''Very.'' She disagreed with people who said you should compromise with life. Her faith wouldn't let her willingly make a bad decision and throw away the future by marrying the wrong man.

''What about you? Stella told me that there were plenty of eligible women who would be very happy to be Mrs. David Ardell.''

''But you're not one of them,'' he said lightly, as if teasing her.

The conversation was beginning to make Melissa uncomfortable. She pulled her hand from his.

They walked a little farther along the bank, but their earlier harmony was lost. ''I think we should get back to the boys before they decide to come looking for us.''

David nodded and called Scruffy back from his sniffing explorations.

They had a quick breakfast and were on the road again within an hour. Melissa doubted that the boys would be at their best when they met their aunt for the first time later that night. Tired, and probably cranky from the long day's travel, it wasn't likely they'd make the best impression. If David hadn't been along, she would have taken an extra day, but she knew he was anxious to deliver them and head back to Denver.

She tried to entertain the boys as best she could by pointing out windmills, some Black Angus cattle, spotted horses and a small flock of sheep grazing on one of the grassy hills. They made a game of seeing who could "I Spy" something different out the window.

David was the one who surprised them when he slowed the car and pointed to a herd of tan-and-white animals, smaller than deer, on a nearby hill. "Antelope."

"I've never seen one before," Melissa said, craning her neck for a better view.

Much to her surprise, David stopped the car on a pull-out where an access road led across the flat ground in the direction where the herd was grazing. "There must be thirty of them."

The boys were scrambling over each other and the dog in the back seat, trying to see out the back window, when Richie had a better idea. "I go look," he said, and reached for the door lock and handle.

"No! Don't open the—" Melissa cried too late, as the back door swung open, Scruffy beat Richie out of the car.

The dog jumping from the parked car alerted the animals, and in a split second the antelope were on the run—with Scruffy in pursuit.

"Scruffy! Scruffy! Get back here!"

The dog ignored their frantic cries as if some lingering strain of heredity had fired his determination to round up the fleeing animals.

Even as they watched dumbfounded, the herd of antelope and Scruffy disappeared out of sight over the next rolling hill.

"Scruffy's gone. Scruffy's gone," the boys wailed loudly. "Come back, Scruffy. Come back."

"Blasted dog," David muttered. Why on earth had he stopped the car in the first place? In a weak moment, he'd given in to a stupid impulse to show the boys some antelope, and look what had happened.

"What'll we do?" Melissa asked, not having the faintest idea how far or how long the dog would chase the antelope before giving up.

"Well, there's no way he can catch up with the herd, that's for sure," David answered shortly. "Antelope are fast and can outrun almost anything. If the dog has any sense he'll give up in short order."

"I guess we'll just have to wait for him to come back," Melissa said.

David didn't answer, and she knew there was a limit to the time he'd be willing to spend waiting for the dog to reappear.

"He's lost," wailed Richie.

Nearly an hour went by, and still there was no Scruffy.

"We got to go find him." Eric set his little chin and glared at David.

"Maybe we should hike a little ways in that direction," Melissa suggested. Anything would be better than just sitting and waiting for the dog to show up.

"All right, but we're not going to put in the whole morning hiking up and down these hills."

They all got out of the car and calling the dog's name as loudly as they could, they walked in the direction that the dog had disappeared.

No sign of Scruffy.

As the midday sun beat down on them, their eyes began to blur from the strain of staring at the surrounding hills for some sign of the pet.

"This is ridiculous," David said, wiping his brow. "No telling how long he kept up the chase."

"Why don't we go back to the car, and just drive a few miles down the road. Maybe we'll meet him coming back."

He looked at her as if she couldn't be that naive, but he nodded. "All right. But if we don't find him in the next hour, we're going to leave him. Agreed?"

The boys howled a protest, but Melissa reluctantly nodded. Even though she hated to think about abandoning Scruffy, she didn't know what else they could do. She knew they could spend the whole day waiting and looking but never find him in these wide open spaces.

David drove slowly down the narrow road that ran along the bottom of the hill where the antelope had been grazing, before they disappeared with Scruffy in pursuit. The terrain was one rolling hill after another,

and when David stopped the car, Melissa feared that
he was going to give up and turn the car around, but
instead he craned his neck and stared upward.

"What is it?"

"See that bunch of rocks on top?" He pointed to
a high plateau. "Maybe we can see something from
there. Let's hike up and take a look." He turned to
the dejected little boys. "I'm sorry fellows, but if I
don't see some sign of the dog from the top of that
hill, we're leaving. Understand?"

They nodded, but both of them held their little
mouths in stubborn lines. They all piled out of the
car, and the boys bounded up the slope of the hill like
mountain goats, while Melissa and David climbed after them at a slower pace.

When they reached the outcropping of rock on the
highest point, a panorama of rolling treeless hills and
wild grassy plains spread out in every direction. Melissa's breath caught at the spectacular view of vast
uninhabited space that stretched to the horizon. Nothing relieved the seemingly endless grasslands and oc-
casional rock formations. No farms, ranches or
houses.

They shaded their eyes with their hands and
searched the landscape. Nothing. No movement of
any kind.

"Where's Scruffy?" Eric demanded with childish
impatience, as if he'd expected to find Scruffy at the
top of the hill, ready to jump on them with wet kisses.

Melissa moistened her dusty lips but couldn't find
any words to reassure him. Her silent prayers to find
the dog had gone unanswered. David moved off the

rock on which he'd been standing, and she expected him to admit the search was at an end, but he didn't.

"I'm going to check something out," he told her. "I want all of you to stay here. I mean it! Don't be wandering off. I sure don't want to spend the rest of the day hunting for one of you."

"What is it?"

"Probably nothing."

He started walking in a diagonal direction down the hill. With every dusty step, he chided himself for being foolish enough to prolong the inevitable. He wanted to find the dog so badly that he was giving in to hallucinations. A moment before, when he'd let his eyes play over flickering patterns of light and dark below them, he'd thought he glimpsed a moving form. The impression was so quick and nebulous that it was gone before he could focus on it. It was probably a trick of his own vision or a moving cloud's shadow upon the ground, but he knew he'd never forgive himself if he didn't investigate.

As he came down the hill to the spot that had caught his attention, he could see some flat boulders in a jumbled heap. Even before he reached the rocks, he was ready to admit that his imagination had provided an illusion of movement, but as he came closer, a muffled sound reached his ears.

He stopped. Listened. Tried to identify the sound. Cautiously, he approached the rocks that were piled up in a way that provided meager shade. He stiffened as he saw something move, and was ready to jump back quickly. Then he saw two familiar, sorrowful eyes looking at him from the protective shade of a leaning rock. Utterly collapsed and panting heavily, Scruffy lifted his head wearily and then let it drop again. His tail barely flickered in recognition.

"You stupid hound," David said in a tone that was both affection and exasperation. He knelt down beside Scruffy. "Come on, get up! Let's get out of here. You've cost us half a day already."

Repeatedly he tried to urge the dog to his feet, but Scruffy wasn't having any of it. There wasn't an ounce of energy left in the dog's body, and his chest heaved with labored panting. When David eased him out from under the rocks, he just went limp.

"It's all right, boy." David stroked him. There was no doubt that Scruffy was in bad shape. The dog had almost run himself to death. Undoubtedly his whole body was dehydrated, and David knew that he'd never make it on his own up the hill and down the other side to the car. Unless they wanted to abandon him, there was only one answer.

David groaned just thinking about it.

Melissa had tried to keep track of David as he made his way down the hill, but when his lone figure blended into the landscape, she lost sight of him.

The boys kept up a steady chorus of questions about Scruffy and David's whereabouts.

She gave them cryptic answers as she kept scanning the hillside below. When David finally came into view again, she realized that her fingernails were biting into hands because they were clenched so tightly.

"Oh, no," she breathed in disappointment. There was no sign of a dog following at his heels as he slowly climbed the hill toward them.

His bulky figure looked strange and his walk was labored. At first her mind didn't register the truth. Then a cry burst from her chest when it hit her. He was carrying Scruffy on his back, the limp dog's legs draped over his shoulders.

When he reached them, instead of running forward, Eric and Richie backed away, terror in their eyes as they stared at the limp dog.

Melissa chest tightened. *Please, dear Lord, don't let him be dead.*

David dropped to his knees and eased the dog from his shoulders. Scruffy made an effort to get up and then collapsed, lying motionless with his legs stretched out flat like a bear rug.

"What's the matter with him?" Melissa asked anxiously. Her relief that the dog wasn't dead was suddenly overshadowed by fear over his alarming condition.

"He just about ran himself to death. The mutt must have chased the antelope herd until he collapsed. Then he managed to crawl under the shade of some rocks. It's pretty likely he would have died of exhaustion and dehydration, if by some miracle I hadn't caught a glimpse of him."

She closed her eyes in thankfulness. Although David would never admit they had been led to this very spot, she knew better.

"What's the matter with Scruffy?" Eric demanded as he eased forward with Richie peeking around him.

"He's just tired. Once he gets some water and some rest, he'll be fine. David found him in time." She smiled at him, her eyes filled with grateful tears.

Then she leaned over and impulsively kissed his dusty cheek. "Thank you."

"I just didn't want to spend the rest of the trip listening to a lot of weeping and wailing," he said gruffly, trying to deny the pleasure her happiness and kiss gave him.

"We found Scruffy. We found Scruffy." The boys began chanting, hopping around in glee.

"We'll get him back to the car and get him some water." Then David eyed the sky. "Looks like an afternoon storm is brewing north of us. Just what we need to make this a perfect traveling day!"

"It's a happy day," she corrected him. "You were right. It was a miracle that we found him."

Chapter Seven

David's hopes to make up time once they got back on the main highway quickly faded. They had to stop at the first place they could, to get water for Scruffy and fill a bottle to take with them. Although the tired dog's thirst began to be satisfied, he required additional stops because of drinking all that water.

The boys were fussy and irritable. Tired from the trek up and down the hills, and uncomfortable crowded in the back seat with the sprawling dog, what they really needed were naps. Melissa tried putting Richie in the front seat while she sat in the back with Eric and the dog, but that didn't work. They were just as fussy as ever. Her own reserve of calm composure was depleted after the ordeal Scruffy had put them through, and when she started seeing billboards advertising places to stay in the next large town, she decided that all of them had had enough for one day.

Even though there were several hours of daylight left, she leaned forward and told David in a firm voice, "I think it's time to stop for the night. There's no sense going on when we're all exhausted. We can have an early dinner and then hit the sack. Frankly, I'm not in the mood to put up with two fussy kids any longer than I have to."

He tightened his jaw. "I wanted to get as close to Yellowstone as we could so we could drive in early tomorrow, spend a few hours and head on to Wolfton." He didn't add that he'd have to turn around and head right back to Denver the next morning in order to make an important appointment with the Senate chairman. What a fool he'd been to think he could get away for even a couple of days.

"We could skip going into the park," she said, wishing that she'd never planned the extra excursion.

"It's too late to change our route now. We'd have to backtrack to go around Yellowstone." He glanced in the mirror, and when he saw the pained expression on her face he felt guilty. Just because he was under pressure to get the trip over with, didn't mean that she and the kids should suffer. No one had forced him to come along. The fiasco with Scruffy wouldn't have happened if he hadn't stopped the car. "All right. We'll find some accommodations and call it a day."

Melissa would have settled for an economy motel, but David pulled into a luxurious resort with a swimming pool and landscaped gardens bordering a golf course. An attendant took Scruffy to an enclosed area, with his own doghouse and patch of lawn. The boys might have made a fuss about leaving him if the dog hadn't plopped down beside bowls of water and food, and gone to sleep.

A bellhop escorted them to two deluxe rooms on the second floor with wrought-iron balconies overlooking an inner courtyard. Each room had two double beds, a sitting area and glass doors leading out on the balcony. Melissa was grateful for the iron railings when the boys bounded about like scouts checking out new territory.

David said he'd meet them downstairs in half an hour, and disappeared into his room. Melissa maneuvered the boys in and out of the shower, and grabbed a quick one for herself. In fresh clothes, revived and hungry, they joined David in the elegant dining room.

As they waited to be shown to David's table, Melissa was glad that she'd changed into a blue linen summer dress and matching sandals, and had caught her dark hair in a twist at her nape. She'd even touched her lips with a soft pink gloss. She was a little amused because she almost felt as if she were on a date, even though she was holding hands with two coltish boys.

Eric's and Richie's faces were clean and shiny, and their rebellious hair neatly combed. They wore clean knit shirts and shorts, and Melissa had wiped off the dust from their only pairs of shoes.

David stood up as they came across the room toward him. His hair was still damp, and dark blond strands lay softly on his forehead as he smiled at them.

''You guys clean up pretty good,'' he teased as he held out chairs for all of them.

The boys were amazed by the spacious dining room. David suspected that they had never eaten in such a place in all their young lives, and they looked small and vulnerable sitting in the dining chairs. Both of them stared openly at the formally dressed waiter who hovered around them, and when David asked what they wanted to eat, they were suddenly mute.

Melissa ordered baked chicken and French fries for the boys because they'd enjoyed that when Inga had fixed it. She was pleased that even in such a short time, regular meals had put some meat on their bones and fleshed out their shallow cheeks. She was sure that with good nutrition, Richie would probably be a stocky child, while Eric's slender body structure would always carry less weight. Her heart swelled with affection as she looked at them.

David saw the tender softness in her eyes and a spurt of protectiveness surprised him. He didn't want to see her hurt. Clearly her emotions ran deep in her quest to find a home for the boys, and he feared that she was heading for heartache. It was a long shot that Paula Bateman could be persuaded to take two active kids to raise, even though they were blood relatives. He sighed inwardly, knowing that the boys probably should have been turned over to Social Services in the beginning. He wanted to honor Jolene's wishes, and he'd do his best to make certain that the children didn't lack for anything, but he and Melissa might have no choice but to go through government channels to place them. Just delaying the inevitable wasn't good for anyone.

Melissa had made it clear that she was in no position to raise them alone. Apparently there was no man in her life who offered her the kind of marriage she wanted. Obviously she had no intention of keeping up any contact with David once the boys were placed—and it was just as well, David told himself. He'd had his heart broken once. He wasn't open to inviting that kind of hurt again.

Melissa caught smiling glances from other diners at nearby tables who seemed approving of the young family they appeared to be. How easy to give the wrong impression, she thought. She knew David's mind really wasn't on the polite conversation they had during dinner, and that he'd probably be up half the night working again. It wasn't any of her concern, but she couldn't help but resent the fact that he couldn't get away for even a couple of days without demands being made on him. She wanted to challenge the mad merry-go-round that left no time or space in his life for anything but worldly pursuits, but she knew he would just mock her naiveté.

As they left the dining room, they passed an expensive gift shop, and the boys stopped short when they saw some colorful children's cowboy hats and boots. Melissa knew the prices would be exorbitant and tried to pull them past the window, but Richie hung back, staring longingly at a pair of rust-colored boots about his size.

David glanced down at the old shoes that the boys were wearing. Their mother had probably picked them up at a thrift store, he thought. He hadn't paid much attention to Richie's and Eric's clothes, but he suddenly realized that Melissa must have bought some of them at her own expense. He was mad at himself for not noticing, and irritated with her for not saying something.

He jerked his head toward the shop's door. "Come on, fellows. Let's see if they have a couple of pairs of cowboy boots your size."

Melissa nearly swooned over the price tags, but by the time they left the shop, the boys were outfitted in cowboy boots, hats and fringed leather vests. Melissa thought David seemed as pleased with the purchases as the boys, as they strutted in their new duds down the hall ahead of them. Maybe men always remained little boys at heart, she mused, pleased to catch a glimpse of this side of the usually staid David.

"What time are we heading out tomorrow?" she asked him as they paused at her door. She knew that he'd be pushing hard to cover as much distance as possible.

He frowned, obviously mentally calculating the trip that lay ahead of them. "How about a six o'clock wake-up call, and we can get away by seven?"

"Fine," she agreed, knowing that if he were alone, he'd have hit the road hard and steady, but the handicap of two kids and a dog had tossed his timetable to the wind. "I really appreciate what you're doing."

"What *I'm* doing? You're the one." His voice was suddenly husky. "You're a very special person, Melissa. I've never known anyone quite like you." He searched the deep calmness of her ocean-blue eyes. "Don't you ever think about what you want out of life and go after it?"

"Of course I do. And sometimes I want things to

be the way I want them, *right now*," she admitted with a sheepish chuckle. "Then I soon find out that the timing was all wrong, and I wish I'd had more patience and trust."

He just shook his head. "I don't believe that anything is accomplished by waiting around. If you don't work hard and stay on top, you never win."

"It depends upon what prize you're after," she said. With a deep sense of sadness, she knew that they were miles apart when it came to understanding each other.

After the boys were tucked into bed, prayers said and one short story told, Melissa quietly slipped out on the balcony to try to unwind from the day's activities. She could hear the ringing of David's telephone next door, and she knew that she was right in her earlier assumption.

The evening air was cool, and she hugged her robe tightly around her as she leaned against the balcony railing. The indigo night sky was speckled with stars, and there was only a sliver of a new moon. She spent several minutes in quiet meditation, as she drew on a sense of oneness with the magnificent heavens and the divine Creator.

David's light was still on when she slipped back into the room and went to bed. In spite of her unwillingness to think about him, she couldn't stop wishing that things were different. Her confession to him about being too impatient to wait for something had been an honest one. More than once, she had ignored intuitive warnings and bolted ahead, only to reap the fruits of her impulsiveness. Never one to lie to herself, she admitted that her feelings for David had deepened. The more she was with him, the more she wished he might have been the one to share her life. Maybe taking this trip together had been a mistake, she thought as she tried to ignore a deep sense of loneliness that she hadn't felt before.

The next morning, they had two grumpy little boys on their hands. Waking them up early enough to fit David's schedule did little to ensure the right mood for a long day in the car. Scruffy was rested and ready for something aside from sleep, but neither Eric nor Richie would put up with his licking and tugging. They fussed at the dog and at each other.

"Eric's on my side!"

"The dog won't get off me."

"Tell Richie to move over!"

David shot them a quick look over his shoulder. "Simmer down, cowboys."

"Melissa," one of the boys wailed, but she didn't say anything or turn around. She'd already tried gentle persuasion to get them interested in something other than fighting, but without any success. She was curious to see how David would handle the situation. The boys were quiet for a few miles, and then the squabbling began again.

Melissa swallowed back a snicker when David raised his voice in a thick western drawl. "I reckon I'd better be letting you drive, Melissa, so I can join them two cowpokes in the back seat. Sounds like they be riding for a fall."

There was a weighted silence in the back.

"How about it, partners? You want some help figuring out what the trouble is?" David looked into the rear mirror at two wide-eyed little boys who were shaking their heads. He winked at Melissa as the low murmur of boyish voices replaced their earlier squabbling.

Late in the morning, the bright sunny weather gave way to dark clouds gathering on the northern horizon. As gusts raced across the open prairie, David tightened his hands on the steering wheel to keep the car steady against the wind's battering.

"Wow, when the wind blows around here, you'd better batten down the hatches," Melissa exclaimed as she watched prairie tumbleweeds race over fields and across the highway. Wire fences were already clogged with the prickly dry weeds.

A brown haze rose from nearby plowed fields, and David said, "Looks like some of the farmers are losing their topsoil." As the wind-driven sand clouds grew thicker, they could hear a steady peppering against the exterior of the car.

"Do you think we'll drive out of it?" Melissa asked, as visibility steadily deteriorated. She'd been caught in white-out blizzards in the mountains when the wind drove snow in blinding sheets across the ground, but a sandstorm was something she'd only read about.

He nodded—but there hadn't been any oncoming traffic for miles and he wondered if that meant conditions were worse ahead. He had turned on his headlights, and hoped that any cars coming in his direction had done the same.

Slowing his speed and hunching over the wheel, he kept his eyes fastened on the yellow line of the highway as it appeared and disappeared in dirt clouds rolling in front of the car. A high-pitched shrieking wind and the constant sandblasting against the car frayed their nerves.

Scruffy started whining and moving restlessly from the seat to the floor.

"I can't see out the window," Eric complained in an anxious little voice, perceptive enough to sense the tension in the adults.

"It's just a windstorm," Melissa said as casually as she could. "The wind is picking up dirt and making clouds out of it. Some people call them sandstorms."

"I don't like them," Eric said.

"Me, neither," Richie chimed in. He was sitting quite close to his older brother instead of on his own side of the seat, and was even using the middle seat belt, as if disputes over seat territory didn't count when things got rough. Melissa didn't blame him. She found herself leaning a little closer to David as the wind and sand battered the car. She was glad that she'd risen early enough for her usual morning prayers for guidance and protection.

Any kind of traffic on the road would have been reassuring, but mile after mile they seemed to be alone in the vast emptiness of Wyoming. Melissa had never seen so much open space in her life.

At one point the wind slackened and they saw that they had left the cultivated area behind. No more plowed fields should mean less loose dirt waiting to be whipped into the air.

"Maybe we're out of the worst of it," David said hopefully. His eyes burned from concentrating so intently on the highway markings, and a pain in his neck and shoulders protested his hunched position over the steering wheel. He didn't want to think about how much time they'd lost during the past couple of hours, creeping along at a snail's pace.

Instead of driving out of the storm, they found themselves engulfed in a blinding brown-out; miles and miles of barren land offered no resistance to gale-force winds sweeping across open ground. The highway disappeared in clouds of sand just as a blast of wind hit the car with a tremendous impact.

David tried to compensate for the car's movement sideways, but couldn't. The heavy car began to slide as its tires lost traction in the moving sand.

The ground fell away.

Melissa cried out as the car dropped off the road and plunged downward. All of them were flung forward against their seat belts, and when the car came to an abrupt stop, it pitched to one side.

There was stunned silence, not because anyone was hurt but because of the suddenness of what had happened. Then Eric and Richie began to cry.

"It's all right. It's all right," Melissa soothed as she quickly unfastened her seat belt and climbed over the seat into the back. She let out a prayerful breath when she saw they were safely fastened in. Scruffy was the one who looked a little dazed; he had been thrown off the seat onto the floor.

"Anyone hurt?" David asked anxiously as his gaze traveled over Melissa and the children.

"No. Just scared," she assured him as she unfastened the seat belts and gathered the sobbing boys in her arms. "You're okay. You're okay. Everything's going to be fine. Just fine," she murmured as her worried eyes held David's.

What are we going to do?

He looked away quickly, not wanting to let her see how stunned he was. His relief that no one had been injured instantly faded as the realization of their perilous position hit him.

The wailing of the wind and the relentless barrage of sand against the car was even louder now that he'd turned off the engine. Trying to see anything out of the windows through the thick brown haze was impossible. The pitch of the car indicated that they had slid into a ditch, but he didn't know how deep, or how far off the road, the car had plunged. Venturing outside too soon would be suicide.

His cell phone wasn't any good under the circumstances. It wasn't strong enough to transmit at this distance and in these conditions. Around town it was fine, and he'd never expected to need it in an emergency like this one. He ran a hand agitatedly through his hair as he analyzed the situation.

"What are you thinking?" Melissa asked, needing to share whatever thoughts he was having, even if they weren't the most reassuring.

He kept his voice as even and steady as he could. "As soon as the wind settles down, we'll be able to see how to drive out of here, or I'll go for help."

Go where? Melissa silently asked. They both knew that the closest highway facilities were still miles away, because they had checked the map when they made plans where to stop for lunch. Plans that were now a mockery. As a quiver of panic threatened to overcome her, Melissa reminded herself, My protection comes from on high. She began to mentally draw on all the scripture verses promising that God's grace was always with her.

As the torturous minutes ticked by, the wind kept up its fierce attack. David became anxious that if the winds didn't abate pretty soon, blowing sand could bury the car and make it impossible to get the doors open. As he listened to Melissa's efforts to counter the boys' fears with stories, songs and prayers, he wondered if she fully realized the danger facing them.

It didn't help to know that *he'd* put their lives in jeopardy. He should have stopped before the winds got so fierce, but he had stubbornly stuck to the decision he'd made on how far they would get by nightfall. Now, all of that seemed insignificant. What did a few extra hours or even a day really matter? It hadn't been worth the risk. He knew that anyone but Melissa would have been berating him for his stupidity. At all cost he had to get her and the boys out of here safely.

For hours they remained trapped in the car, waiting, listening and watching for any sign that the dust storm was over. When Eric and Richie finally fell asleep in the back seat, Melissa climbed into the front seat with David.

He avoided looking at her. Admitting his mistakes

had never come easily for him. All his life he'd tried
to live up to his parents' expectations, fearful of losing their love. Now, he was sure that he'd destroyed
any positive feelings Melissa might have had for him.

"Quit blaming yourself," she said with insight. Impulsively she took his hand and gave it a reassuring
squeeze. Then she leaned back against the seat, closed
her eyes and kept her hand in his as the minutes
ticked by with excruciating slowness.

David kept glancing at his watch. The afternoon
was nearly gone when the sound of whipping wind
lessened and the brown haze outside the windows
grew thinner. Were they going to be trapped here all
night? Would the car be almost buried by morning?

David was afraid that his senses might be betraying
him, but when Melissa sat up and raised a questioning
eyebrow, he knew that she had noticed the subtle dif-
ference in the wind, too.

"I think it's letting up," she said softly.

He nodded and took the first breath of relief he'd
had in hours. The responsibility for getting them into
this mess rested heavily on his conscience, and he was
ready to do anything to make sure that they came out
of the experience safely.

At first, they couldn't see clearly through the wind-
shield, but gradually it became apparent that the car
rested at the bottom of a ravine. David felt his chest
tighten, knowing that it would be impossible to drive
the car back up that kind of steep slope. And the
chances were infinitesimal of anyone seeing the car
at the bottom, covered with sand.

"I'll have to get back to the highway and stop someone."

"We'll all go."

"No," he said firmly. "It's still bad out there. You and the boys are better off here."

She knew he was right, but just sitting there waiting wasn't going to be easy. No telling how long he'd be gone.

"I'll have to tie something over my nose to keep the sand out."

"Here, take this." She pulled off the soft scarf that she had used to tie back her hair. Quickly, she put it over his nose and mouth and knotted it at the back of his head. "There. You look like a highwayman," she said lightly, trying not to let him see how vulnerable she felt as he prepared to leave her alone in the car.

He pulled her into his arms, gave her a long hug and said in a muffled whisper through the scarf, "Don't worry. I'll be back with help."

When he tried to open the door on the driver's side, he discovered that the car was snugged up tightly against a bank of dirt and rocks and the door would open only a crack. Even before he could get it closed again, a gust of wind sent sand flying into the car.

Melissa tried the passenger door and it opened more easily, but it took David's strength to move the sand piled against it and open it wide enough for him to slip out.

As the blast of air invaded the car, Scruffy gave a *woof,* leaped over the front seat, and was out the door before David could slam it closed again. When David turned and disappeared through the thick haze, Melissa couldn't even tell if the dog was at his heels.

As she felt a trembling rising within her, she closed her eyes and repeated the ninety-first psalm until the words brought her a calming assurance. "...because you have made the Lord your refuge...no evil will befall you...for He will give his angels charge of you to guard you in all your ways."

Chapter Eight

The air was thick with sand whipped by a lingering wind. Fortunately David's dark glasses protected his eyes enough to keep them open. Melissa's scarf protected his nose and mouth. As he lowered his head and started up the ravine's rocky slope, Scruffy darted around David's legs, nearly tripping him.

"Down, down," David ordered in a voice muffled by the folds of the scarf. He couldn't believe it! That's all he needed: to try to keep track of a dog. He knew that the winds could build up again at any moment, and he couldn't afford the time to get Scruffy back in the car. He had no choice. He had to make use of the small window of partial visibility, and get up to the highway. The dog was on his own. Why on earth had he ever agreed to bring the mutt along in the first place?

In some places, David had to climb upward on all fours. Wild coarse grass and sticky weeds cut into his hands. Drawing air through the layer of cloth over his nose and mouth made his breathing labored. Despite the glasses, his eyes were scratchy from dirt getting under his eyelids. The car had dropped so quickly, he couldn't judge how far it was to the top. A sporadic wind was still creating a brown fog all around him.

Scruffy bounded recklessly at David's side, repeatedly bumping against him as he tried to rub his face against David's arms and legs to clear his dust-filled eyes. Sometimes the dog pushed so hard that he almost caused David to lose his balance on the sliding rocks and earth.

"No, no," David ordered.

When the dog suddenly left him, David felt both a sense of relief and worry. Because his focus had been on the ground under his hands and feet, he had no idea whether the dog had dropped back or gone ahead.

David let out a muffled "Scruffy."

No response. Maybe he'd gone back to the car. Was Scruffy smart enough to scratch on the door for Melissa to let him in? In any case, trying to locate him in the murky fog was impossible.

David shoved concern for the dog behind the compelling need to get help for Melissa and the children before the storm's reprieve was over.

As David continued to struggle upward, a frightening thought made him stop in his tracks. He paused, squinted upward, but couldn't tell what lay beyond a scattering of wild bushes. Panic overtook him. Had he been moving sideways on the hill instead of straight up to the highway?

David stood there, frozen, trying to make some

sense out of the terrain, when suddenly he heard Scruffy's insistent bark. What now? thought David in exasperation. Was the dog lost on the hillside? Needing rescuing again? His irritation began to lessen when he realized that the barking was coming from somewhere above. Could it be that Scruffy had already reached the top of the hill and the highway?

Guided by the dog's barking, David scrambled over jagged rocks, climbing upward until he pushed through scratchy bushes and suddenly found himself on the shoulder of the highway.

Scruffy jumped on him with a welcoming yelp, and David hugged him. "Good dog. Good dog. Thanks, fellow."

With Scruffy bounding at his heels, David walked out in the middle of the highway and looked in both directions. The road was still shrouded in brown fog. His heart sank. No sign of any car lights. The only sound was the wailing wind. He knew that anyone used to this kind of dust storm would know better than to venture out on the road when the visibility was so poor.

What to do now?

He told himself that if the winds continued to abate, there was bound to be some traffic eventually. But how long would that take? When he thought about Melissa and the boys cooped up in the car, hungry and frightened, he clenched his fists in anger at his helplessness.

He walked a little way in one direction with Scruffy at his heels, and then in the opposite direction. He couldn't see any sign of human habitation on either side of the road. Even though visibility was improving, he was careful not to leave the place where the car had gone off the road. There was nothing around to serve as a marker. No trees. No signs. How would he ever find the exact spot again? He had no choice but to stay in the same place until help came.

He paced and paced, and when a faint white spot finally appeared in the distance he jerked off his dark glasses, not knowing what he was seeing. Then, as a vehicle took shape, he let out a shout that set Scruffy barking.

A highway patrol car.

David raced to the middle of the road and stood there, waving and shouting. As the patrolman braked to a stop, David ran over to him and started shouting, even before the man had a chance to roll down the window.

"My car," he shouted. "It's down there. I've got people inside."

"Calm down," the middle-aged patrolman ordered. "Get in the car, and take that thing off your mouth so I can understand what you're saying."

Melissa heard voices and David's shouts even before his face appeared at the dusty window. She had put the boys in the front seat with her, and let them take turns behind the steering wheel. They made up a game of pretending where they were going, and the children were enjoying the fantasy. She was the one who had to deal with reality as the minutes passed.

In her mind's eye she tried to visualize what was happening, but finally gave up and kept her focus on believing in answered prayer. When the long vigil came to an end and she opened the door to David and a man in a trooper's uniform, grateful tears spilled down her cheeks. *Thank you, Lord. Thank you.*

David stiffened when he saw the tears. "Are you all right? The boys?" he asked anxiously.

She wiped away the happy tears and assured him, "We're fine."

"Where's Scruffy?" Eric demanded in an accusing tone. David's return obviously wasn't his highest priority.

At the sound of his name, the dog jumped into the car and began laying sloppy kisses on the two giggling boys and Melissa.

"Come on. We've got a climb to make," David warned.

Clearly, the patrol officer had expected to find a tense situation, and he looked a little bewildered by the high spirits and laughter inside the car.

As Melissa, the boys and dog climbed out of the car, David said, "This is Officer Mackey. He's got a patrol car waiting to take us into the next town."

"I can be calling for an ambulance if you'll be needing one," he said.

"No, there's no need," Melissa said quickly. "You're an answer to our prayers, Officer."

His eyes crinkled in a responding smile. "I'm thinking you've had more than a little blessing today."

"I guess we gave the Lord a workout, for sure," she agreed.

The wind had diminished to a light breeze, the air

was clearing, and the position of the car at the ravine was clearly visible. Officer Mackey surveyed the hillside where the car had slid off the highway. "It's hard to believe that the car didn't turn over on the way down." He shook his head. "No way a wrecker can get this baby back up that steep slope."

Until that moment, David hadn't given any thought to how they were going to get the car out of the gully. His attention had been on getting help. Now the impact of the situation hit him. "You mean, there's no way to recover the car?"

"I didn't say that," Officer Mackey said as he let his brown eyes rove up and down the gully in both directions. "Could be there's a way to bring a wrecker in from the other side. There's a county road that runs along this ravine a little ways back. Might be they could come in that way." He eyed David. "Going to cost you some, though. They'll have to remove some rocks and clear a track. A lot cheaper than letting this baby turn to rust."

David nodded. "That's for sure. How long would something like that take?"

The patrolman shrugged his broad shoulders. "Hard to tell. If Tom Yates Towing can get right on it—no more than a day, I'd say."

David's stomach took a sickening plunge. What was the governor going to say? Another extra day could risk the appointment that had been promised him. "How far is it to the next town?"

"About fifty miles. You're lucky my run this afternoon brought me in this direction. We always get a bunch of stranded travelers in dust storms like this, but usually there's nothing to do but wait out the storm on the side of the road." He looked as if he was ready to give David some advice, and then thought better of it. "Well, I'd better be checking in before they send another unit to follow up on my call." He gave Eric and Richie an appraising look. "You fellows good at climbing?"

"We're real good!" Richie boasted.

"We climbed a big, big hill when Scruffy was lost," Eric said.

The patrolman's eyes twinkled. "Sounds as if you've had yourselves an exciting trip."

Before the boys could start relating Scruffy's escapade, Melissa told them to get what they needed out of the back seat. The first things they grabbed were their cowboy hats. There was no way they could carry all the suitcases, so they chose a couple of overnight bags, and Melissa and David strapped on a couple of backpacks. David took the heaviest overnight bag, and Officer Mackey took the other one.

Now that the skies had cleared and a late-afternoon sun bathed the earth, they could see the easiest path up the hill to the highway. They made the climb in half the time it had taken David.

The patrolman placed a small red cone on the shoulder of the highway to mark the place where the car had gone off. "We'll check the odometer on the way back to get the exact mileage," he told David.

Settled in the back seat of the patrolman's car with the boys, Melissa drew a deep, relaxing breath. David sat in the front seat, and Officer Mackey called ahead and reserved a couple of rooms for them in the Homestead Hotel. The officer said it was the only place he knew that allowed pets.

"Right downtown, it is," he assured them. "Nothing fancy. Rents out rooms by the night, week and month. Nice little café just around the corner. You and the missus should be real comfy there."

Melissa waited for David to correct him, but he didn't. She decided that either David didn't think it was important to set the record straight, or he was getting used to people jumping to the wrong conclusion. She secretly liked the idea of giving the impression that they were a family. If there were a way their relationship could become more permanent, she would welcome him into her life, but the truth of the situation was undeniable. All of David's energy was focused on the vision he had for his career. She'd glimpsed the world in which he lived and knew that she didn't belong in it. Not now. Not ever. And one thing seemed certain: he wasn't going to change. She had tried to bring up any discussion of spiritual beliefs several times on the trip, but he sidestepped them with all the finesse of a successful lawyer.

Now he looked tired and preoccupied. No doubt he was wondering what else could go wrong. They should have been in Wolfton by now. They would have to call Paula and explain the delay.

Melissa sighed. Her grandmother had taught her to believe in divine right timing, but at the moment she saw nothing good coming out of this forced delay. Her weariness was bone deep, and she looked forward to a nice warm bath that would soak the rigid muscles in her neck and back.

David was relieved to see that the small town was more than just a wide spot in the road. Three stop-lights controlled the traffic on a busy main street that stretched five or six blocks long. When a familiar fast-food restaurant came into view, both boys put up a howl.

"I'm hungry."

"I want a burger."

"Scruffy wants one, too."

With a deep laugh, the patrolman turned into the drive-in. "Well, now, I can't have a couple of starving young'uns on my conscience, can I."

Melissa's own stomach contracted with emptiness as they picked up their two-sack order and promised the boys that they'd eat as soon as they got to the hotel.

"Here we are," Officer Mackey said a few minutes later, as he pulled up in front of a two-story stone building. "You folks make yourselves comfortable now. Just ask the Henshaws for anything you need." He turned to David. "Tom Yates Towing is two blocks down. I'll stop and give him the details, but you'd best be giving him a call yourself. Tom will have to hire some extra help to get the job done."

David nodded. "As soon as we get settled, I'll walk down and talk with him."

As the boys got out of the car with Scruffy pulling at his leash, the officer told Melissa, "There isn't much to do around here to pass the time, but we've got a city park with a nice playground. I'm betting you'll find some friendly kids and dogs running around there. You've got a couple of live wires there.''

Melissa laughingly agreed and thanked him for all he'd done for them.

The Homestead Hotel was well named. The weathered stone building looked as if it had stood in the same spot since Wyoming was a territory. Numerous renovations had only added to its Old West look. The rustic lobby was paneled in knotty pine and furnished more like someone's homey living room than a commercial hotel. The furniture was worn, and several older gentlemen stopped their chatter long enough to give the new arrivals the once-over.

There was a small registration counter in one corner, and a hefty man with graying hair and a close-clipped beard and mustache watched them as they crossed the lobby. His broad mouth spread in a welcoming smile as he greeted them.

''You're the folks that Officer Mackey called about. The wind can sure kick up a fuss around here. Guess you've had yourself a time, all right.'' He wore small round glasses that perched low on his nose, and his eyes fairly danced, as if he could hardly wait to hear all about it. ''Ran off the road, did ya?''

''Yes, we did,'' David responded without elaborating. ''You have a couple of rooms for us?''

''Nothing right together. We only have a few rooms to let. Most of our guests are residential. I've got rooms 4 and 9.'' He peered at them, raising his salt-and-pepper eyebrows. ''Hate to break up a family but that's the best I can do.''

''That'll be fine,'' David said, and indicated he was

ready to sign the register. He put both rooms in his name as he had done the two nights before.

"There's a fenced yard in the back where you can let the dog out. No barking, though."

"No barking," David repeated, as if there were no question about Scruffy's manners.

The rooms were at both ends of the hall, but they were spacious with high ceilings and tall narrow windows. One had a double bed and the other twin beds. Their earlier arrangement of Melissa having the children in her room wasn't going to work. They were going to have to split up the boys. One of them would have to be with David.

Melissa explained. She expected a big to-do, and was surprised when Eric volunteered to make the change. Then the truth came out.

"I'll keep Scruffy company," Eric said happily, knowing that the dog had stayed in David's room during the trip.

David winked at Melissa. "I guess that tells it like it is. Which room do you want?"

"You take the twin beds. Richie and I will do fine in the double bed."

David glanced at his watch, and his jaw tensed. "I'd better talk to the towing people right away. If the patrolman's idea of reaching the car isn't feasible, we'll have to look at some other options."

She knew that he was tired, drained and functioning on pure willpower. Impulsively she touched his face, murmuring reassurances that everything was going to work out. She was startled when he turned his head and pressed a kiss into the palm of her hand.

The soft and gentle touch of his lips brought a warmth to her cheeks.

For a long moment they didn't move, as if some strange chemistry was humming between them, and then Melissa drew away. She was startled by the unexpected physical attraction, and knew that their frightening ordeal had made them both vulnerable.

"You better eat your burger before you go," she said as evenly as she could, avoiding looking at him.

When she wouldn't meet his eyes, he regretted that he had added a new constraint between them. He wanted to explain that he'd given in to an affectionate impulse to show her how very special she was. He hadn't known many people like Melissa who "walked the talk," and any doubts he'd had about the strength of her religious faith had been dispelled by the way she handled herself and the boys during their ordeal.

Even though he had never been drawn to a woman on so many levels, he knew that the hope of developing any lasting personal relationship with Melissa was just wishful thinking. She would never accept his cynical attitude. She'd made it clear that she believed in God's intervention and credited Him with keeping them from harm until they could be rescued. He wanted to argue that all of the happenings could just as easily be explained as coincidences or blind luck. His trained mind wouldn't let him accept what his mother used to call "delusional fantasies."

"I'll be back as soon as I can. I'll take my burger with me. You'll be all right, won't you? Is there anything you need?"

She shook her head. "I'm pretty sure there's one change of clothes around in overnight bags and backpacks. If we don't get our luggage tomorrow, we may have to do some shopping."

He nodded and left, but she knew he was frustrated by his lack of control in the situation.

After eating and bathing, they took Scruffy outside. Melissa was pleasantly surprised. The backyard turned out to be a spacious lot, and the boys and dog took off at a run toward a tire swing hanging from a sturdy oak tree.

A brick fence enclosed a broad lawn and planting of wildflowers that bordered a flagstone path leading to a charming old gazebo. Melissa felt as if she'd stepped back in time as she sat on a bench, watching the children and the dog play. Her love of pioneer history was stirred as she gazed upon the old stone hotel, suspecting that a hundred stories were waiting to be told about the women who had passed by this very spot. If they were stuck here for a couple of days, she'd do a little research.

Eventually, Melissa began to wonder if something had gone wrong at the towing company, and was relieved when David came into view. He spied her sitting in the gazebo, gave her a wave and walked toward her with that long stride of his.

Scruffy bounded over and threatened to trip him with his exuberant welcome. Whether David cared or not, Scruffy liked him, and Melissa was happy to see him laugh at the dog's antics.

"Sorry to be so long," David said as he dropped down on the bench beside Melissa. "Mackey had already contacted the towing company, but the owner, Tom Yates, wasn't convinced that the patrolman's idea about how to reach the car was viable. He called in a couple of the guys that work for him, and they spent nearly an hour hashing the whole thing over before they decided to try Mackey's idea. They'll go out first thing in the morning, but there are no guarantees.''

"The patrolman seemed to think it could be done."

"Well, I offered a good monetary incentive. If they can get the car out of the ravine early enough in the day, we can be on our way before nightfall." He brushed back a shock of hair. "Of course, that's assuming that the car isn't damaged in any way. The engine was still running fine when I turned it off."

"Well, there's nothing more you can do about it tonight," she said. "What do you want to do about dinner? I don't think the boys will be very hungry after eating so late in the afternoon."

"I don't feel much like eating, myself," he confessed. "There's a small café a few doors down the street. I'll watch the boys, if you want to get something."

She shook her head. "Right now, I'd like to call it a day—or maybe a day-and-a-half," she added with a wry smile.

"It does seem like ages since this morning. Time is really relative, isn't it?" His eyes fastened thoughtfully on her face.

"Yes, it's hard to grasp sometimes."

"I can't believe there's a time when I didn't know you. How has it happened, Melissa Chanley, that you've become so much a part of my life in such a short time?''

''I'll have to think about it,'' she answered with an evasive smile. He wasn't being flippant or flirtatious, and his sincerity momentarily threw her off balance.

Just then, Eric and Richie raised a fuss about who was taking the longest turn on the swing. ''Time to put them to bed,'' she said.

David agreed. ''I'm going to hit the shower and then the sack myself. Any advice about tending Eric?''

''I think he'll be fine. You'll probably be awake before he is in the morning. Bring him down to my room if you want to leave early.''

She helped Eric gathered up his night things, gave him a good-night kiss and told him to take care of Scruffy. He nodded and held Scruffy's leash tightly as he followed David down the hall to the other room.

David wasn't quite sure how to handle the ''getting ready for bed'' routine. He was relieved when the boy seemed used to looking after himself. By the time David was out of the shower, Eric was already in his pajamas and in bed, with the dog at his feet.

''All set?'' David asked as he sat down on his twin bed and prepared to turn out the light.

''Don't you do prayers?''

''Do prayers?''

Eric nodded. ''You can go first.''

David had been backed into a corner more than once in his professional career, but never by a kid. ''That's okay,'' he said. ''You go ahead.''

''God likes you just to talk to him. Melissa says

so," Eric explained a little defensively. "But you don't have to do it out loud."

"I understand." David nodded, wondering how to play the part suddenly thrust on him. "Doing prayers" had never been a part of his upbringing, and as an adult he'd never joined a church or made worship a part of his life.

He watched as Eric closed his eyes, clasped his hands and moved his little lips in a silent prayer. When he was finished, he turned to David. "Now, a story."

"It's getting pretty late. I think we'd better forget about any story tonight."

He frowned. "Don't you know any?"

"Sure, I do, but—"

"Melissa always tells us a story," he complained. "She knows lots of them. I like 'Baby Moses in the Basket' best. He needed a new home, just like me and Richie. Do you know that one?"

"I'm not sure," David said slowly. "Why don't you tell it to me?"

"Okay," he said with his shy smile, obviously pleased to know something that David didn't. The way he told the story, the baby's trip down the river in a basket was pretty exciting. David had to question whether some of the extra details that he put in were even in the Bible, but the message was clear. God had found a neat place for Moses to live.

"That's a good story, and you told it very well," David said, smiling. "I guess I can turn out the light now."

Eric frowned. "Don't you do 'good-night kisses,' either?"

"I guess I have a lot to learn about this bedtime business." David chuckled as he bent over Eric's bed and kissed the boy's freckled cheek. "Good night. Sweet dreams."

Eric beamed. "That's what Melissa always says."

David lay awake for a long time, trying to remember a time when his mother or father had kissed him goodnight and wished him "sweet dreams." They were usually gone somewhere, leaving hired help to watch him. He'd never known the gentle sweetness that Melissa showered on the two children who weren't even her own. She believed in a God of love, and maybe what he had said to Eric about having a lot to learn was true. He felt a little foolish wishing that someone would kiss him goodnight and wish him "sweet dreams."

Chapter Nine

"Will you watch the boys for a few hours this morning?" Melissa asked, as they sat at a table in the crowded café, enjoying a home-style breakfast of sausage, hash brown potatoes and pancakes. "I'd like to spend a little time at the local library. There may be some interesting stories about women in this area that I could work into my book." She saw the flicker of a frown cross his face. "Did you have something else to do?"

"I just need to make some phone calls and check in at the office, but I can do that later today," he said quickly, unable to turn her down. After all that had happened, she deserved a little time to herself. He marveled that there was no sign of yesterday's trauma in her manner or easy smile. She continued to amaze him with her ability to adjust and accept a situation that would have thrown most women into a tailspin. "Checking out the library sounds like a good idea."

"Are you sure? I know you're feeling a lot of pressure over the delay."

"I'll get a handle on it," he reassured her, even as he thought of the work piling up on his desk. His secretary would be having a fit, trying to reschedule appointments and fielding all kinds of questions that only he could answer. As soon as they towed the car into town and checked it out, he wanted to get on the road again. He'd leave Melissa and the boys, and head back to Denver as soon as possible.

"Why don't you take advantage of the situation?" Melissa asked him, seeing the tense set of his jaw.

He looked puzzled. "What do you mean?"

"Nobody knows where you are. You could sneak in some free time before they catch up with you."

He smiled and responded to the teasing glint in her eyes. "You're a bad influence, you know that?"

"I know. But haven't you ever had a secret desire to leave everything behind? Run away and join the circus?"

"Me?" He shook his head and laughed. "Never."

"Circus?" Eric's head jerked up from his pancakes. "We saw a circus on television, didn't we, Richie?"

His brother nodded eagerly. "Can we join one, Melissa?"

"Not today," Melissa answered smoothly, as if the question were reasonable enough. "But I'm sure David will find something fun for you to do."

"Thanks a lot," David chided Melissa. With that kind of promise, what choice did he have but to live up to their expectations? "All right, you go do your

thing at the library, and the boys and I will see what
this little town has to offer three fellows on the
loose.''

They left the café and went back to the hotel to
feed Scruffy and put him on a leash. ''Shall we meet
back here at lunchtime?'' she asked.

David nodded. ''Okay, buckeroos, let's hit the
trial.''

Melissa couldn't help but chuckle as she watched
him head down the street with a dog and two boys
clumping along beside him in cowboy boots and hats.
The scene brought a rush of tenderness to her heart
and tears to her eyes.

The time Melissa spent at the library turned out to
be wasted. Even though she found the early history
of the town interesting, she failed to find any refer-
ence to a pioneer woman who might have left an im-
print on the local history because of her strength of
character or convictions. She needed the account of a
truly courageous woman as a lead on her book. Discouraged, she began to question the whole idea of
writing a book about pioneer women of faith. Maybe
it wasn't worth continuing. Even as doubts crossed
her mind, she remembered a favorite saying of her
grandmother's, when Melissa would predict failure
about something. *If you name it, you claim it.*

The memory reminded her that if she decided that
the project wasn't worthwhile, it wouldn't be. She'd
doom it to failure because of her own disbelief. Deep
down, she felt that she was supposed to write this

book, and as she left the library she renewed her commitment to keep searching for the right material.

Melissa glanced at her watch. Nearly noon. She wondered how David had made out as a baby-sitter. Eric had proudly confided in her that he had told David the bedtime story of Baby Moses. Even though she was happy to see that Eric was opening up and beginning to trust David, she was also worried about how the sensitive boy would react when David disappeared from his life the way his mother and father had.

When she returned to the hotel, she found two excited boys who each wanted to talk at once. It took her a few garbled moments to get the story. David had found a pony ride for kids. Broad smiles and sparkling eyes lit up their little faces.

"You should have been there," Eric told her.

"My horse went fast," Richie bragged.

"Mine was the biggest."

"He couldn't catch up with mine."

"Yes, he could."

"Okay, fellows," David said in a tone that put an end to the mine's-better-than-yours argument. "You both did a good job."

"You let them ride real horses?" Melissa couldn't quite believe what she was hearing.

"Yep." David winked at her. "And if they hadn't been going around a circle in that corral, they would have been streaking across the prairie like real cowboys after a runaway steer. Right, guys?"

Eric and Richie waved their cowboys hats and yelled, "Hip! Hip! Hooray!"

"You didn't think I was up to this kid-watching business, did you?" David said, grinning.

"You set a pretty high standard," Melissa admitted, laughing and shaking her head. "I'm afraid taking them to the park this afternoon is going to be a letdown."

"The park?" Both boys looked at David and whined, "You promised. You promised."

"Promised what?" Melissa asked, afraid to hear the answer. At this point, she didn't know what to expect. David was suddenly full of surprises.

He gave her an apologetic look. "I guess I promised that you'd take them to a movie this afternoon."

"Can we go, Melissa? Please?"

Relieved that the promise was one that she could keep, she said, "Sounds like a good idea."

Before they left the hotel, Melissa called Paula's number, and a recording machine clicked on. Melissa left a message that they hoped to arrive tomorrow afternoon, and they'd call again if plans changed.

After putting Scruffy on a leash in the backyard with water and food, they had a quick lunch at the café. David planned to return to the hotel to work while Melissa took the boys to the movies, but as they left the restaurant she decided to see if she could change his mind.

"I think you ought to come with us. When was the last time you slipped off to an afternoon movie?"

"Well, not recently," he answered smoothly, when the truth was that he couldn't remember when, if ever, he'd neglected work or school to go to a movie.

"Maybe it's time," she said. "You might like it."

He had opened his mouth to tell her he couldn't, when a little hand crept into his. Eric smiled and gently pulled at him like someone urging him to join in a game. "You come, too."

Melissa held her breath. This kind of reaching out to someone was totally unlike Eric, and she feared that any kind of rejection could send the boy back into his shell. Would David realize the fragility of the moment and surrender to the little boy's need?

With great effort, David swallowed back all the well-worn excuses that had supported his work-centered life. The feel of a child's hand in his, and a hopeful smile on a grinning freckled face completely disarmed him. He knew it was idiotic for him to spend precious time watching a kid's show when important matters were waiting for his attention. He couldn't believe it when he let himself be pulled along by two joyful kids and a smiling dark-haired woman whose lovely eyes did something to the rhythm of his heartbeat.

A little later, loaded down with popcorn and soft drinks, they sat in the small theater with a crowd of squealing kids and watched the children's movie. At first, David couldn't adjust to the bedlam and the behavior of the uninhibited audience. The clapping, laughing and yelling drowned out the movie's dialogue, but nobody else seemed to pay any attention to the added noise. Everything was in constant motion, and he lost count of the number of times the kids in his row scrambled in and out of their seats.

He sat next to Melissa, with Richie on her side and Eric on his. When he let his arm slip over the back of her seat to lie softly on her shoulders, she didn't seem to mind, and he laughed at himself for feeling like an adolescent again, taking his girl to a Friday night movie.

Melissa was concerned that he wouldn't be able to relax and enjoy himself. A children's matinee was not comparable to a performance of the Denver Civic Orchestra or Ballet Company but as she caught glimpses of his relaxed face and ready smile, she grinned smugly to herself. Maybe there was hope of softening the governor's counselor, after all.

As she leaned closer into the curve of his arm and shoulder, she teased herself with the illusion that the real world would not be waiting for them when they walked out the theater doors.

"We're close enough to walk over to the towing garage and see what's happening with the car," David said, after the film ended. The owner had told him it would be late afternoon at the earliest. He had warned David that he wasn't sure their plan to reach the car was even feasible. It all depended on whether they were able to find a way into the ravine that would allow them to tow the car back to the road. If not, he said, David might as well forget the whole thing and count the loss.

As they approached the garage, David's pulse quickened. The Lexus was already parked outside the garage. "Look. There it is! Maybe we can get out of here today, after all."

The magic of the movie's fantasy faded abruptly when Melissa saw the instant change in David. Smile lines around his mouth and eyes disappeared, and she could tell from his expression that he was already focused on making up for lost time.

The boys hung back, staring at the dirt-covered car with apprehension. Melissa had the same reaction. Just seeing it brought back vivid memories of the hours they'd spent hearing the lashing wind and blasting sand.

As David started toward the door of the garage, Melissa said, "We'll see you at the hotel."

"All right. I'll call you if I'm going to be delayed." He gave them a wave as he disappeared inside the building.

How quickly his holiday was over, she thought sadly. He was already looking ahead to resuming the frantic pace he'd set for himself. She wondered if he would recall the afternoon he'd spent at the movies with fondness—or guilt. As she walked back to the hotel between the two boys, Eric tugged at her hand.

"Can't we stay in this place?" he asked, looking up at her with an old-man worried expression. "I like it here."

"Me, too," Richie added.

Their innocence tugged at her heart. Only children could see life in such simple terms, she thought, and her voice was husky as she tried to explain that they hadn't finished their trip yet. "If the car is okay, we'll have to leave here in the morning."

She'd already decided that there was no way they were going to push and drive anywhere this late in the day. They all needed a good night's sleep for the last day's journey through Yellowstone and the final hundred miles to Wolfton. When they reached the ho-

tel, she let the boys play with Scruffy in the yard for
a few minutes before she put them down for a late
nap.

Taking her daily meditation book out to the gazebo,
she sat in quiet contemplation, praying for guidance
and giving thanks for the Lord's protection.

The boys slept for about an hour, and woke up
hungry. Just as she was wondering how much longer
David would be gone, he joined her and the boys in
her room, carrying two large carryout sacks.

"I thought eating in would be easier than going out
somewhere. We've got a full day tomorrow, so we'll
need to get the kids down early."

"I take it that the car's in working condition."

"You bet," he said happily. "It's hard to believe,
but the slide down that rocky hillside didn't damage
a thing. After the guys carefully checked the car all
over and gave it a wash and wax job, you'd never
know it had been buried in a gully. I guess we were
lucky all around."

David could call it luck if he wanted to. She'd
never believe it was luck that had kept them safe and
brought them help.

They left the hotel and were on the road early the
next morning. It was only fifty miles to Yellowstone,
and Melissa could tell that David wasn't going to
spend any more time than was necessary to satisfy
her. He was probably thinking that if she hadn't insisted on going through Yellowstone in the first place,
they would have taken a different road and would
have avoided the sandstorm altogether. But she didn't

see any point in letting the unfortunate accident spoil this part of the trip.

"We are going to see a lot of real animals," she told the boys. "Not just pictures."

"Bears?" Richie asked, his eyes wide.

"Maybe not bears," Melissa admitted. "But I bet we see some deer and buffalo, and maybe even a bull elk with antlers this big." She held out her hands to show the wide span of a full-grown elk.

"What are antlers?" Eric asked, frowning.

David suppressed a smile. He couldn't fault Melissa for wanting to educate the boys, but reaching them on their level might be a bit of a challenge. She patiently tried to answer their questions, and he was wondering why she hadn't pursued a teaching career. He wasn't at all convinced that she should be spending her time working on a book that had limited commercial value, but he knew better than to question her decision. She seemed as set on her vision of what she wanted out of life as he was on his.

He had mapped out their trip so they would take the east entrance into the park, make a circle trip to get a view of the lake, Old Faithful geyser and some of the wildlife, and then exit at the west entrance.

Melissa was in awe of God's magnificence as they traveled deep into the natural setting of forests, cliffs and rushing waters. The beautiful color of Yellowstone Lake was almost indigo, she thought as she stood on the bank and watched it rippling toward the shore.

"Are there fish in there?" Eric asked David, peering intently into the water.

"Probably lots of lake trout."

"Can we catch some?"

He laughed. "Not today."

"But sometime?" Eric persisted.

"Maybe," he said, avoiding Melissa's frown. They both knew that there was little chance of repeating the fun the boys had had fishing for their dinner.

David kept a tight leash on Scruffy. Loose pets were not allowed in the park. When they stopped a little later to view a herd of elk resting in a meadow close to the road, they made certain that Scruffy didn't pull his usual trick of bolting out of the car while the door was open.

Melissa insisted that they take the boys on the boardwalk that overlooked the thermal springs steaming out of the earth.

"They look like Inga's teakettle," Richie said excitedly, pointing to the hot white clouds of steam.

Melissa laughed and winked at David. "You're exactly right, Richie. Steam is coming out of the earth the same way that it comes out of a teakettle."

They had lunch in a lodge that had been built near Old Faithful. They sat on benches that circled the area, and when white foaming water blasted hundreds of feet into the air, Melissa jumped up and squealed, "See, see, there it goes."

David laughed and circled her waist to keep her earthbound during the few minutes of the spectacular display. Eric and Richie watched quietly. Apparently bigger wasn't better as far as the boys were concerned. They were a lot more enthusiastic about the steaming "teakettles" and "bubbling mud pots."

David looked at his watch after the geyser had disappeared, and said firmly, "It's time we headed north if we're going to get to Wolfton this afternoon."

"I know," she said regretfully. "Thanks for being so patient and sharing this beautiful park with me." She knew she would store the memory in her heart for a long time. She'd never forget the beautiful scenery, but part of that cherished remembrance would be the warmth of the man and the children who had briefly been a part of her life for this wonderful day.

They reached Wolfton about three o'clock in the afternoon and were surprised at the size of the mountain town. A welcoming sign at the city limits informed them that it was the county seat.

There was a western charm about Main Street that gave it the ambience of a small community, while it showed every sign of being a bustling little city. Paula had given Melissa simple directions about how to reach her place, and on the way, she caught glimpses of houses scattered along the steep slopes of the mountain and thick stands of evergreen trees. She was disappointed that Paula's home was so isolated.

Richie and Eric were unusually quiet, and when she glanced in the back seat she could tell they were fearful of another change in their young lives.

"It's going to be all right," she assured them with a bright smile. "Your aunt Paula is going to love you."

"What if she doesn't?" Eric asked with his usual bluntness. "Do we have to stay?"

"No, of course not," Melissa said, as if they had

some choice in the matter. "But we're going to have a nice visit."

A brightly colored mailbox with a carved wooden blue jay on top stood at the bottom of a curved driveway.

"Nice place," David said as he parked at the bottom of a flight of stairs leading up to the log house's redwood deck. He gave a couple of toots on his horn, but nothing happened.

"Maybe she didn't hear us," Melissa said, wondering why she was so nervous.

"Well, let's announce ourselves." He gratefully stretched his long legs and walked around the car to open the doors for Melissa and the boys.

Scruffy bounded out of the car with his usual exuberance, and for a change, nobody yelled at him. The dog seemed to be the only one filled with enthusiasm about having finally arrived at their destination. Eric and Richie hung behind Melissa and David as they walked to the house, acting more like victims than two little boys coming to visit their aunt.

David didn't see a doorbell, and when he opened the screen door to knock, he saw a note taped to it: "Gone for a walk. Come in and make yourselves at home. Paula."

"I guess she got tired of waiting for us," David said as he tried the front door. When it opened easily, he turned to Melissa. "I say we take her at her word."

Scruffy didn't wait for any further discussion; he slipped past David into the house. As if the boys were waiting for that kind of reassurance that everything was okay, they darted in after him.

Melissa laughed as she slipped her arm through David's. "I guess we've arrived, ready or not."

Chapter Ten

"I feel funny about coming in when she's not home," Melissa said in a hushed voice, as if someone was around to hear them invading. Even the boys were nervous as they looked around, and stayed close to Melissa. Scruffy seemed to be the only one totally at ease. He began sniffing his way around the place, as if he were in charge of deciding whether they should stay or not.

"Let's wait to unload the car until she gets here," David said. "In the meantime, we'll be polite guests and not disturb anything—right, boys?"

Richie whispered anxiously, "Does she have a potty?"

"I think we can find one." Melissa motioned for him to follow her down the hall to a small bathroom opposite the staircase. Wide-planked floors and a beamed ceiling stained a rich walnut color harmonized with a colorful Indian and western decor in furniture and wall hangings. A staircase mounted the wall at one end of the room, and a center hall led to a roomy kitchen and back patio that overlooked the valley below and surrounding mountains. Everything about the home was warm and inviting.

Eric was the one who discovered a pan of cookies sitting on the stove. Melissa decided the aunt must have baked them as a welcome for the boys, so she let each of them have one.

The boys were happily playing with their cowboy figures in front of the fireplace, when the sun began to fade behind the nearby peaks. There was still no Paula, and David and Melissa exchanged questioning looks. The note had said "a little while," and they had been there a couple of hours.

When the telephone rang, David quickly picked it up. "Hello, Bateman residence."

"Who's this?" a man's gruff voice demanded. "I was wanting Paula."

"I'm sorry, she's not here. We're waiting for her."

"Are you the one bringing the kids?"

"Yes, I'm David Ardell. I'm here with Melissa Chanley and the two boys. May I ask who this is?"

"Jim. Jim Becker. Let me talk to Paula."

"She's not here, but she left a note on the door saying that she'd gone for a walk and would be back shortly."

"What?" He gasped. "You mean, Paula hasn't come home yet?"

"No, not yet. We've been here a couple of hours."

"That note was on the door yesterday when I dropped by to check on things."

''Maybe she posted the note again when she went for another walk this afternoon.''

Silence. ''Is there a pan of cookies still out on the stove?''

''Yes,'' David said. He felt a sudden cold ripple up his spine.

''She hasn't been back.'' He slammed down the phone.

David slowly replaced the receiver and stared at it.

''Who was that?'' Melissa asked, puzzled. She didn't understand why David had hung up without even saying goodbye.

''It was Jim Becker, asking for Paula.''

''I heard you tell him that she'd gone for a walk. Is something wrong?''

''I don't know,'' he answered as he walked over to the front windows. *She hasn't been back.* The man's words kept repeating themselves in his head like the harsh clang of a warning bell. If Paula had left yesterday afternoon for a walk, where was she now?

Melissa came up beside him, searching his tense profile. ''What is it? What's wrong?''

He quietly repeated the conversation he'd had with Jim Becker. ''There could be a hundred explanations for the note still being on the door. Maybe she didn't take it down yesterday or she put it back up this afternoon.''

As she searched his face, her chest suddenly tightened. Had Paula been gone over twenty-four hours? ''Where could she be? What could have happened?''

''At this point, everything's a guess. No good

jumping to conclusions until we have more to go on. She could have stopped off to visit with a friend and let the time get away from her.''

''I suppose so,'' Melissa said without conviction.

Melissa swallowed hard as an uneasiness rose to the surface. ''It's almost dark, and the note said she'd be back in a little while. What do you think we should do? Should we alert someone, like the police?''

David knew that a person had to be missing twenty-four hours to be put on a missing person's alert, but if what this Becker guy said was true, Paula had been gone since yesterday afternoon.

''I think that this Becker will call in her disappearance,'' David said. ''He seemed really worried. Let's just stay put and see what happens.''

A few minutes later a flash of car lights hit the front window. Both David and Melissa breathed a sigh of relief. ''Someone's here,'' he said.

The front door flew open and a young man burst into the house. He had dark hair caught in a ponytail and was dressed in jeans and a plaid shirt.

''She come in yet?'' he demanded with obvious agitation.

Both David and Melissa shook their heads.

''I dropped by yesterday morning when she was baking. When I came by the house in the afternoon, she wasn't here.'' He waved the note in his hand. ''This is the same one that was on the door yesterday afternoon.'' There was an edge of accusation in his worried tone.

David said quietly, ''We had no way of knowing that she hadn't put it there just a little while before we got here. There was no reason for us to be concerned. We thought she'd be back momentarily."

"Yes, of course." Jim took a deep breath. "How would you know the note has been on the door since yesterday?"

David held out his hand. "I'm David Ardell, and this is Melissa Chanley."

"I'm Jim Becker." He introduced himself as if he'd forgotten he'd already given his name on the phone. "I was a lodger with Paula until about six months ago, when I got on the fire department and had to move into town. Then I married Nancy and haven't been paying as much attention to Paula as I should have."

After making certain that there had been no change in the kitchen since the day before, he called 911 and reported her missing.

Eric and Richie were still sitting on a rug with their toys, not saying anything and watching with big eyes.

"These her two nephews?"

"Yes, this is Eric and Richie." Melissa smiled reassuringly at them. "Eric is six years old, and Richie is almost five."

"Paula was pretty excited about them coming for a visit. That's all she's been talking about. She knew you were arriving today, didn't she?" he asked.

Melissa replied, "She expected us yesterday afternoon, but I called and left a message that we'd been delayed and would be here today."

Jim swung on his heels. "Her answering machine is on her bedroom phone." He turned and bounded up the stairs.

David and Melissa followed him into a large front room that was obviously a combination lady's bedroom and sitting room. A small lady's desk flanked by bookshelves stood in front of a picture window overlooking the small town below. The telephone answering machine on the desk was blinking.

Jim pushed a green button and a mechanical voice said, "You have one message."

When Melissa heard her voice on the recording, her stomach took a sickening plunge. *Paula had not picked up yesterday's message.*

"She must have already been gone from the house," Jim said in a worried tone. "What time did you call?"

"About twelve-thirty, when I got back to the hotel from the library. Maybe she just didn't erase the message," Melissa offered in the hope there was some simple explanation.

"Why would Paula put the note on the door yesterday afternoon if she hadn't been expecting you then?" Jim countered with a frown.

They reasoned that Paula had probably already left the house before Melissa tried to telephone to advise her that they were going to be delayed a day. That meant she had left the house before twelve-thirty yesterday.

Jim glanced out the windows, where darkening shadows were beginning to creep across the landscape, warning them that the sun was already sinking behind the high mountain peaks.

"They'll be rounding up a search party, but we

can't do much more than check the area around the house tonight.''

"Where else would she go?" Melissa asked, utterly bewildered by the sudden crisis. She couldn't believe that they had been comfortably passing the time waiting for Paula, when she might be in some kind of danger.

"Hard to say. Paula loves hiking. She's been traipsing all over these mountains since she was a child. I've been hard put to keep up with her when we've been out together. If she took a walk, you can be sure it was more like a hike." His forehead wrinkled in concern. "Some kind of trouble found her or she'd be here, spunky as ever."

"Does Wolfton have an adequate police force?" David asked. How efficient could the law enforcement be in a town this size?

"Paula's house is in the county. It'll be the sheriff and his deputy in charge."

David didn't find this news very reassuring. He knew from experience that county law officers were overworked, with too much jurisdiction to do the best job.

"There's a mountain rescue unit in town. I'll notify them and call in some help on my own," Jim said, sitting down at the desk and starting to dial.

David and Melissa went back downstairs and found Eric and Richie waiting at the bottom of the stairs. Melissa knew she had to explain the situation to them—but how?

Before she could collect her thoughts, Eric said angrily, "She ran away, didn't she. She doesn't want us and that's why she ran away."

"No, it's not that at all," Melissa said, taken aback by his vehement tone. She hadn't realized that such a fiery rage seethed under the surface of his quiet manner.

"We don't like her even if she makes good cookies," Richie added pugnaciously, taking his cue from his older brother. "We want to take Scruffy and go."

"Your aunt did not run away because you came to see her," David said firmly, and Melissa gave him a grateful look. "Come and sit down, and we'll explain."

"Why do we have to stay here?" Eric demanded as the boys trailed David across the room.

"For now, we all have to stay here," he answered, knowing that he was included. His plans to leave in the morning would have to be put on hold by this latest development. "Your aunt is missing."

"Like the lady at the church said my mother was missing?" Eric asked. "Is Aunt Paula in heaven, too?"

"What?" David asked, looking totally puzzled.

"I'll explain later," Melissa told him as she sat on the sofa with the boys beside her and tried to explain. She wondered how her voice could sound so positive when inside she was reeling from the sudden nightmare that had such tragic possibilities.

While they talked, Jim came downstairs and started pacing the living room floor. When a car pulled up in front of the house, he dashed to the door and jerked it open to let two men into the house.

"You've got to get a search party going right away, Sheriff," Jim said without preamble.

Both men were dressed in tan uniforms. The sheriff was a sandy-haired man, fortyish, with thick shoulders and a large-boned frame. The deputy was a young man with a stocky build and muscular arms. They both had tense and unsmiling expressions.

The sheriff's sharp eyes fastened on Jim's face. "The report said Paula's been missing since yesterday. How do you know that?"

Jim thrust the note into his large hand and repeated his story about having seen it pinned to the door the day before. Then he nodded at Melissa and David. "She was expecting these folks yesterday, but they got delayed. They found this note still on the door. That means—"

"You're sure it's the same note?"

"Yes," Jim said firmly. "It was fastened on the door the same way, in the same spot—"

"All right," the sheriff conceded. "Maybe she left the note on the door two days."

"What about the kitchen and the cookies? Nothing's been changed since yesterday morning. She hasn't been here, I tell you." Jim's voice rose, and the sheriff put a firm hand on his shoulder.

"Calm down. It won't do anybody any good to panic." He turned to David and Melissa, and let his sharp gaze slide over the boys. "You're Paula's kinfolk?"

"The boys are," David said. He introduced himself and Melissa. "What can we do to help?"

"Not a heck of a lot right now. I've got a call out

for a search party. As soon as they get here, we'll check out some of Paula's favorite spots.'' Even as he spoke, another car pulled up in front of the house.

''It's Judge Daniels,'' the deputy said, peering out the window.

''That figures. Zackary Daniels has been sweet on Paula as long as I can remember. I wouldn't be surprised if he didn't close up court the minute he got whiff that she was missing.''

Judge Daniels was a well-built man with pleasantly balanced features and a beard and mustache. When Jim let him in, he asked anxiously, ''Is it true, Jim? There's a missing report out on Paula?''

Jim nodded and explained that she'd probably been gone since the day before.

''How in the blazes did that happen and nobody knew?'' he demanded almost angrily.

''Easy, Zach,'' the sheriff said in a warning tone. ''We'll figure this thing out. You know how Paula is. No telling what she got in her head to do before company got here.''

The judge's worried eyes swept over David and Melissa, and settled on the boys. He forced a smile. ''These little fellows must be the kinfolk Paula was telling me about. Richie and Eric, I believe she said their names were.''

Melissa nodded, surprised when he introduced himself as Zackary Daniels, omitting his title. ''Most everyone calls me Zach.''

There was an obvious touch of affection whenever he said Paula's name, and the sheriff's remark about Judge Zackary Daniels being sweet on her seemed to be the truth. Obviously not willing to let another minute go by without deciding on some course of action, he turned to the sheriff and demanded, "What's the plan, Sheriff?"

"We'll have to wait until daylight to make any kind of a thorough search. The foothill behind the house is about all we can safely do this time of day. In another hour, you won't be able to determine what's a rock and what's a tree, let alone anything else."

"We should check out Chimney Rock tonight," Zach insisted. "That's one of her favorite hikes and it's not far from the house."

Three more men arrived with an attractive woman with curly blond hair who looked to be in her thirties. She wore a sloppy pullover and faded jeans, and had a bounce to her steps as she came right over to Melissa and the boys, greeting them with a broad smile that showed a dimple on her round face.

"I'm Carol Carlson, the reverend's wife. Paula told me all about your upcoming visit." She beamed at Eric and Richie. "What sweet boys. I have two little girls about your ages who would just love playing with you."

"That would be nice," Melissa said quickly, trying to make up for the boys' scowls and turned-down mouths as they glared at the woman.

"Shall we go in the kitchen while the men get themselves organized?" she said in a way that told Melissa that Carol Carlson had probably taken charge in this kind of tense situation more than once. "I brought a little something for a quick supper so you don't have to fix anything.''

"That's very thoughtful of you,'' Melissa said gratefully. Her own stomach was so tight she hadn't thought about eating, but she'd bet the boys were more than ready for supper.

Carol directed Melissa toward the right cupboard to get the plates and glasses. "I know Paula planned to use her good china, but under the circumstances I think the everyday service would be better.''

For the first time, Melissa heard a falter in her voice, and sensed the strain she must be under to keep everything upbeat and positive. "You and Paula are good friends, aren't you?''

She nodded. "When my husband, Skip, and I came to Wolfton, neither of us knew anything about serving a church. I would have been lost if Paula hadn't befriended me.''

"Do you know where she might have gone yesterday afternoon?''

Carol was silent as she began to uncover her casserole dishes. One was a baked chicken potpie with a golden crust and the other a deep-dish apple cobbler. "I talked to Paula yesterday morning, and she didn't say a thing about going anywhere. She was all excited about getting the boys' room ready for them. Do they like the cowboy bedspreads?''

"We haven't been up to the bedrooms yet. We were waiting to unload the car until she got back.'' Melissa worried her lower lip. "We kept thinking she'd be back any minute. We didn't know she'd been gone since yesterday.''

They heard the men leaving, and a moment later David came into the kitchen. He had hung back, listening to the men, wanting to offer to join them but knowing that he'd be more of a liability than a help. They didn't need someone stumbling around blindly on the side of a hill while they looked for Paula. "I feel like a fifth wheel in this situation. I'm afraid a paper-pushing lawyer isn't much good in a crisis."

"Sometimes we just don't know what our role is," Carol told him, smiling. She glanced at him and then at Melissa as if wondering about their relationship.

"David was a friend of the boys' mother," Melissa said, and then explained how her connection with Eric and Richie had developed through the homeless shelter. "The two of us have been working together to find a new home for the boys."

"I see." Carol nodded her approval. "Well, sit down. We'll thank the Lord for our blessings and put Paula in his care."

"Amen," Melissa said softly, and was startled when both Eric and Richie chimed in "Amen, amen, amen," as if they had decided that if one "amen" was good, a few more were even better.

Neither David nor Melissa did justice to the delicious meal, and both were unusually quiet, but Carol didn't seem to notice. She paid a lot of attention to Scruffy and listened attentively as Eric and Richie talked at once, telling her about the dog running away after the antelope.

When it was time to clear the table, Carol said, "I'll just pop the leftovers in the frig. There's coffee, toast and cereal for breakfast. Paula probably intended to make fresh biscuits and sausage gravy, her favorite,'' Carol said with an obvious catch in her throat.

"What do you think has happened to her?" David asked as kindly as he could. It was obvious there was a close tie between the two women. As a lawyer, he knew the value of listening and asking questions.

"I think Paula took one of her hikes and got into trouble. What kind, I don't know."

"Could she have gotten lost?"

"No, not Paula. She knows these mountains like the proverbial back of her hand."

"Then, something unexpected must have happened. A fall? A wild animal?"

"I don't know," she said, "but I believe in angels, and I know one of them is watching over her right now."

Melissa nodded at Carol. "'He will give his angels charge over thee','' she quoted. "We'll keep Paula in our prayers and the Lord will bring her home safely."

David managed a smile but disbelief was in his eyes.

"I'm sorry I can't stay," Carol said, after the kitchen was in order. "I'd better get home and collect my daughters from the neighbors. Skip can catch a ride home with someone."

David walked out to the car with her. They stood for a moment, searching the darkness of the hill behind the house. Lights like giant fireflies flitted among the trees as the searchers made their way upward.

"How will they ever find her on a mountain as big as that one?" David asked quietly.

"There's an outcropping of rocks about halfway to

the crest where Paula likes to sit and view the valley below,'' Carol explained. ''It's a hard climb for someone not in condition, but I know she's hiked a lot farther than that many times. If the note said she'd be back in a little while, I don't think she planned on going too far.''

''Is she impulsive?''

''Sometimes,'' Carol admitted. ''More now than she used to be. But you'll like her, I know you will.'' On that positive note Carol got in her car and gave David a friendly wave as she drove away.

He began to unload the Lexus. He knew that there was no way he could head back to Denver as planned. A trip that had seemed simple in Denver had turned into a complicated snarl. The hope of persuading Paula to keep the boys seemed farther away than ever, and what was worse, they might have pulled Eric and Richie into another heartbreaking situation. The kids had already been tossed about from pillar to post, and he was less than optimistic that Melissa and he had done them any favors bringing them here.

There were three bedrooms on the second floor aside from Paula's. Cowboy-patterned bedspreads on twin beds identified the boys' room, and their missing hostess had obviously furnished the other two bedrooms for guests or lodgers like Jim.

Melissa was grateful for David's help as they got the boys settled in for the night. She was surprised when he even stayed around for a short story and the boys' bedtime prayers.

Without any prompting, Eric added to his usual prayer, ''Please bless Aunt Paula.''

Richie's prayer was a little more direct. "Please find Aunt Paula and make her like us."

Leaving a small light on in the room, Melissa and David went back downstairs with Scruffy trotting at their heels. The emotional drain of the past few hours had taken its toll on both of them. They sat down on the couch together, Scruffy at their feet.

"I wish there was something we could do," she said wearily as she looked around the living room. The missing woman's presence was everywhere. Her creative touch was on the decorated pillows, colorful knitted afghans, gaily mounted pictures and rows of delicate potted plants that provided evidence of Paula's loving care. A book lay open on one of the end tables as if she'd put it down in haste. Melissa blinked back a sudden wash of tears. *Where are you? Why aren't you here in your lovely home?*

"Steady now," David said softly as he drew her close and she rested against his chest. She felt small and fragile nestled against him, and as he stroked her soft hair with one hand, he felt her tremble.

"I can't believe this is happening. I keep thinking there's some simple explanation that we're missing."

"I know," he said, letting one finger lightly traced the soft curve of one ear. "Everything has happened too fast. There's nothing we can do but wait it out."

She closed her eyes, feeling the rise and fall of his breathing, and comforted by the soothing touch of his hands on her skin. His gentle stroking calmed her nerves and relaxed her tense muscles. She didn't re-alize how close she was to falling asleep until he placed a soft kiss on her forehead and whispered, "Time for bed."

She reluctantly lifted her head and moved away from him.

"You won't do anybody any good if you don't get some rest," he said gently as he eased her to her feet. "Go on to bed."

"What are you going to do?"

"Take Scruffy out for a walk."

"Don't you go wandering off," she ordered. "You're not thinking about joining the searchers, are you?"

"Not *tonight*."

The way he said it, she knew then that he had no intention of being left out of the search if Paula was still missing in the morning.

"Good night, then." She leaned up and impulsively kissed him on the lips. His arms suddenly tightened around her and his mouth captured hers in a breathless kiss that sent a wild spiral of warmth through her. When he released her, she couldn't meet his eyes, bewildered at how a simple good-night kiss in the midst of such upset could turn into something so wonderful.

Chapter Eleven

Melissa awoke with a start, just as the first ray of gray light lined the edges of the bedroom drapes.

Men's voices.

She sat up, straining her ears. Were some of them just coming back from their all-night search? Or were they leaving again?

She dressed quickly and hurried out into the hall, as David came out of his room. His hair was tousled from sleep, and he was still fastening the buttons on his shirt as he came toward her.

"Do you think they found her?" she asked anxiously.

"They gave up the search about midnight," he said as they hurried downstairs together. "Jim said they'd be back here about dawn with a full-scale search party. I guess they've arrived."

She was surprised when David stopped her at the top of the stairs. Putting his hands on her shoulders, he searched her face. "Are you going to be all right?"

She was warmed by the concern in his eyes. "Yes, I'll be fine."

"This waiting isn't going to be easy."

"I know. Waiting never is." She sighed. "I'd much rather be hiking all over the mountain and using up my nervous energy. I guess I'll just have to find some way to keep the boys and me busy."

"Don't go off somewhere on your own. I want to know that you're all safe and sound inside this house."

"Don't worry. We're not going anywhere."

"Keep a tight leash on Scruffy. There will be search dogs running around, and I don't want him taking off to parts unknown."

She felt the corners of her lips curve in amusement. The way he was firing orders at her revealed more than casual feelings for her, the boys and the dog. He almost sounded like a husband and father.

The smell of coffee teased their nostrils as they entered the crowded kitchen. Several men were huddled over a relief map spread out on the table, marking out sectors for several groups of searchers. When Jim saw David and Melissa come in, he reached for the coffee percolator and filled two cups for them. It was obvious that he felt at home in the kitchen, and came and went as he pleased. Deep worry lines in his face showed how much he cared about the missing woman.

"Jim, what can we do to help?" Melissa asked quietly.

"I don't know. Mr. Shornberger from the Mountain Rescue Service is taking charge." He nodded toward a robust man with a ruddy complexion, dressed for mountain climbing.

David moved closer to the table, and after listening to the exchange of ideas between Mr. Shornberger, the sheriff, Zach and the others, he decided that the search was in good hands.

"We'll have to sweep both sides of Prospect Point," the sheriff said. "Paula's been known to hike all the way down to Beaver Lake."

"She's a fool about taking pictures of wildlife down there," someone agreed.

Zach grumbled. "Last week she was climbing all over the place trying to get some snapshots of a couple of eagles. I warned her that she could take a fall— but did she listen to me?" He gave a sheepish grin. "The only authority I have around here is in the courtroom."

As they continued to mark out the map, fear was almost palatable in the kitchen. They went over every possibility of what might have happened to keep Paula away from her home all this time.

When Carol came in with her minister husband, Melissa was surprised and pleased to meet him. She never would have taken Skip Carlson for a man of the cloth. He was tall, had the graceful movements of an athlete, and was dressed more like a lumberjack than a preacher with his heavy pants, checkered shirt and hiking boots. He gave David and Melissa a slow, friendly smile that immediately dispelled any worries they might have had about treating him differently than anyone else.

"This is terrible, isn't it," he said, shaking his

head. "Paula's known for doing her own thing. But who would have thought she'd have the whole town worried about her?"

He chatted with them for a couple of minutes until the sheriff told Shornberger, "There're about a dozen men milling around in the front yard, waiting to be told what to do. I think we've got a good team."

"All right, let's see how many patrols we need," Shornberger said, rolling up the map. "We'll cover the area as best we can."

Before he left the room, David approached him. "I don't know the terrain, Mr. Shornberger, but I'd like to help."

"You that city guy Paula's been expecting?" His sharp eyes traveled over David's expensive chambray shirt and tailored slacks, and down to his brown leather oxfords. "Some kind of a lawyer, aren't ya?"

David nodded. "I work at the Colorado State Capital for the governor."

"Well, fancy lawyering isn't going to do us much good about now," he answered shortly. "And we don't have time to spend watching out for someone who could get lost himself."

"Of course not," David answered evenly, refusing to let the man's dismissive attitude get to him. "But there must be some details of the search that have to be handled from this end. An extra pair of hands and legs ought to be of some use, wouldn't you think?"

Shornberger's ruddy face crinkled in a slight smile. "You're a lawyer, all right. Okay, there are about a half-dozen houses like this one that are perched on the side of this mountain close to Paula's. We contacted as many as we could last night. You can help by hiking up those private roads and chatting with the people who live in these mountain homes. Maybe Paula mentioned something to one of them that will give us a clue as to where she might have gone or remember something that will help. With luck, someone might have seen her before she took off. We haven't had time yet to really get the news out to everyone in the valley, and we need to talk with as many people as we can." Then he added briskly, "It'll free another man if you take over this job."

"I think I can handle it," David said, refusing to take offense at the man's attitude. He knew that everyone was tense and under pressure.

The search party formed into groups, and when they were ready to leave, Skip Carlson held up his hand and immediately the gathering fell silent. They bowed their heads as the minister uttered a simple prayer of thanksgiving for God's presence and guidance. Skip asked for heavenly protection for all those who were giving of themselves in this moment of need, and prayed for a successful ending to their search. "Thank you, Lord. Amen."

Then Shornberger waved his hand, and the men moved forward in their assigned patterns and began their search for any sign of the missing woman in the rugged terrain of trees, rocks and thickets.

"Can you stay with Melissa?" David asked Carol, as she stood on the front deck with Melissa. "I don't think she should be here alone all day."

Melissa started to protest, but Carol cut her off. "I agree. As soon as the girls wake up, my neighbor will

bring them here. The phone will probably start ringing off the wall once the news gets out. I promise
you, we'll have more company and food than we
need.'' Her eyes twinkled. ''Our church ladies just
wait for a chance to compete with each other when it
comes to showing off their cooking skills.''

''What are you going to do?'' Melissa asked David, when it became obvious that he didn't intend to
stay at the house with her and the boys.

''You'd better hurry if you're going to join one of
the groups,'' Carol warned him.

''I'm not.'' David gave a rueful laugh. ''My offer
got turned down. Shornberger gave me another job.
He wants me to check the houses on this side of the
mountain and see if Paula might have said something
to any of the residents that would help find her.''

''Sounds like a good idea. I warn you, though,''
Carol said with a teasing grin, ''some of the women
will talk your leg off just to keep a handsome guy
like yourself around for a little while.''

''He's used to having women make a fuss over
him,'' Melissa said. ''We went to a fancy state dinner,
and David was the most eligible bachelor in the whole
crowd. You should have seen the way the women
looked at him.''

''Not true,'' he said, a slight flush rising in his
cheeks. He'd never been able to take teasing very
well; his upbringing had always demanded a sensible,
no-nonsense attitude. But something had changed.
He'd changed. And he'd laughed more since Melissa
and the boys had come into his life than he ever had
before. The way she was smiling at him made him

want to land a kiss on those full tempting lips, and give Carol something to tease about.

"I'll reserve judgment," Carol said, as if she'd caught the way he was looking at Melissa. "In any case, watch out for Madelyn Delange. She's the second house up the hill, and would love to tell you all about her reign ten years ago as Big Sky Beauty Queen. She's a divorcée and sets a mean trap, so watch out."

"Warning noted," David said, smiling. "Would she be likely to know anything about Paula's activities?"

"She might. Paula gets along well with her neighbors," Carol told him. "There are several scattered houses on this side of the mountain besides Paula's. When you see a mailbox and a driveway, you know there's a house in the trees somewhere high on the side of the mountain. There are some other side roads that were left years ago by loggers, but they're pretty much grown over."

"Don't get lost," Melissa said, trying to deny an insidious feeling of uneasiness about his going off alone. In the past few days he had become an integral part of her, his comforting presence giving her a sense of well-being. She was tempted to ask Carol to watch the boys so she could go with him, but after what Carol had said about the women making a fuss over him, she'd just sound jealous if she indicated wanting to tag along.

David saw flickering apprehension in Melissa's forced smile. He surprised her by giving her a light kiss on the forehead. "I should be back in a couple of hours," he reassured her. "Don't worry."

Carol eyed the Lexus and said, "You'd better take Paula's Jeep. There are some pretty steep driveways leading up to some of the houses. Almost everyone around here uses four-wheel-drive vehicles."

"What about keys?"

"Oh, Paula always leaves them in the ignition. She claims it's easier than hunting all over the house for them."

David just shook his head. This must be the only place remaining in the world where people left their house unlocked and keys in the car. He waved to them after he backed the Jeep out of the garage, then headed up a climbing narrow gravel road that led to other scattered homes on the mountainside.

Carol looked at Melissa with unabashed curiosity as they went back in the house. "Are you two...?"

Melissa laughed. "A couple? An item?" She shook her head. "No, we don't have that kind of personal relationship."

"Really?" Carol said in surprise. "You could have fooled me. I thought I saw a lot of personal feelings mixed in with what you were saying, and not saying, to each other."

"It's complicated."

"Love always is."

Melissa frowned.

"Oh, I forgot," said Carol. "We're not talking about love. Or anything personal like that."

"Would you like to hear the whole story?" Melissa asked. She might as well satisfy Carol's curiosity right up front. In a way she was grateful to be able to share her feelings with someone. How had her desire to help two little boys turned out to be so complicated for her emotionally?

"I'll whip up eggs and toast, and we can have some breakfast before your boys get up," Carol said as they went into the kitchen. "I bet Paula laid in a good supply of everything for your visit."

There was a poignant silence, and then Melissa said prayerfully, "God willing, I look forward to meeting her."

As they ate, Carol listened attentively to Melissa's account of the unusual circumstances that had brought Eric and David into her life and into David's home.

"I could love David, maybe I already do love him," she confessed. "But I can't see a future for us together. The fact that we're not spiritually compatible is a big obstacle."

"How does he feel about it?"

"About what?"

"A future together. Don't you talk to each other?"

"Not about feelings or spiritual things."

"Maybe you should. I was an unbeliever until Skip got hold of me. Then the Lord took the blinders off my eyes—and here I am, a preacher's wife!" Carol laughed. "Talk about God working in mysterious ways!"

Their quiet breakfast was cut short when they heard Scruffy barking upstairs. "I guess the boys are up," Melissa said, pushing away from the table. "I'd better get upstairs before they need a referee."

"And I'd better check on my girls," Carol said,

heading for the telephone. "I'll have my neighbor bring them over so they can play with Eric and Richie. They're all about the same age. Holly just turned six, and Sarah is four."

Melissa tried to prepare the boys for the arrival of their new playmates, but her enthusiasm fell on deaf ears. Both boys gave her a disgusted look. "Girls!"

She couldn't help but laugh. In a few years, they'd be knocking themselves out to get noticed by "girls."

Holly and Sarah were diminutive copies of their mother: blond curly hair, lively blue eyes and boundless energy. They completely snowed the boys in the first five minutes. Carol sent Melissa a triumphant smile as the four children settled on the front room rug to play games.

"Let's slip out and have a second cup of coffee on the deck."

They settled in a couple of patio chairs, and Melissa explained that she earned her living as a writer and about her current project.

Carol looked impressed. "Now, that's amazing."

"What is?"

"You've come to the exact place to find the kind of story you're looking for. Paula's great-grandmother! She came west at the turn of the century with her doctor husband. Emma Bateman was a trained nurse and rode horseback with her husband to every isolated cabin in the valley. They were strong in their Christian belief, and when Dr. Bateman died of pneumonia, Emma continued to go anywhere she was needed to nurse the sick. She even managed to raise a son, Paula's father, all by herself. There are families all over this area whose lives were touched by her dedication. 'An angel on horseback,' they called her.'' Carol cocked her pretty head to one side. ''How's that for a story?''

Melissa looked at her in awe. She felt like a treasure hunter who had just come upon a lode of gold. ''It's perfect. Exactly the kind of story I needed as a beginning chapter for my book. Thank you, thank you.''

''Don't thank me. What is it the Bible says? 'Trust in me and I will direct your paths'?''

''Come on, I'll show some pictures and things that Paula has from her grandmother. She won't mind. I think she even has a diary or daily log somewhere. We'll ask her when she gets here,'' Carol added, as if there was no question in her mind that Paula would soon be home.

David was glad that Carol had suggested his taking the Jeep. A narrow twisting driveway branched off the main road and abruptly mounted upward. Set high on the mountainside was a two-story log home that overlooked the valley. David sat in the car for a minute before getting out. The magnificent panorama was unbelievable as an early morning sun touched high peaks with a crimson glow and lent a velvet patina to green carpets of trees lining the surrounding hills.

David couldn't put the sensation into words, but he felt a stirring deep inside, as if a hidden part of him had suddenly come to life. He wished that Melissa had been there with him. She would have understood.

The silence held an enveloping peace that startled him.

As he slowly got out of the car, the front door of the house opened and an elderly man walked down toward him. The mailbox at the bottom of the driveway had read, The Finleys.

David quickly explained to Mr. Finley why he was there, and from the man's reaction David knew that the news about Paula had not reached her neighbors. The older man was obviously shaken up, hearing about her disappearance, but he couldn't offer any help in finding her. David took his leave as quickly as he could and headed along the side of the mountain to the next home. Driving slowly, he watched on both sides of the road for mailboxes and private driveways cutting through the trees. He was glad that Carol had warned him about Madelyn Delange.

When she answered the door of her spacious Swiss chalet-style home, she was wearing tight white pants and an off-the-shoulder blouse, and her blond hair looked as if she'd just come from the salon. She gave him a welcoming smile even before David introduced himself as a friend of Paula's. She immediately invited him to come inside, but he refused and quickly explained the reason for his call.

When David told her about Paula's disappearance, she raised plucked eyebrows, her eyes widened, and she lifted a manicured hand to her mouth. "Oh, my goodness. Whatever could have happened? You don't think she was kidnapped or anything?" She gasped as if that worry were not foreign to her. "She doesn't have any money."

"Have you seen or talked with her recently?"

She shook her head. "I like Paula a lot, but we're not real close neighbors—you know what I mean? She goes with an older crowd," she added pointedly.

Before David could stop her, she launched into a recital of how busy she was, implying that being the town's social queen was very demanding. She was obviously not concerned about Paula's disappearance but was more worried about a situation that might put her personally in some kind of jeopardy.

David thanked her for her time, refused her invitation to come inside for a cup of coffee and quickly made his escape back to the Jeep. No one was home at several of the houses. Other neighbors were friendly and concerned when he told them the reason for his visit. They had been contacted the night before and wanted to help. But his talks with them ended with the same disappointing results. No one had any information that would help locate the missing Paula.

Discouraged, he turned around in a cul-de-sac where the mountain road ended and headed back toward Paula's house. He hated to see Melissa's disappointment when he told her that he'd learned nothing that would help. His promise to the governor to be back in the office in a couple of days weighed heavily on him. How could he leave her and the boys at a time like this?

He was nearly back to Paula's house when he glimpsed a weather-beaten roof lower than the road and nearly hidden by a bank of rocks and trees. Had he missed seeing a driveway and mailbox?

He braked the car, got out and started walking

down the hill toward the weathered roof. As he broke through the trees, he saw a dilapidated old log cabin facing downhill toward the river. Obviously the place had been abandoned. If there had ever been a road leading down to the cabin, there was no sign of one now. Windows gaped crookedly in its sagging sides and the whole place looked ready to fall in on itself. Relieved that he hadn't missed a house in his enquiries, he turned around and started to hike back up to the road.

At that moment, the unmistakable sound of a whimper reached his ears. He looked around. An animal?

The sound came again. He retraced his steps. He was almost to the front door of the cabin, when the truth hit him.

The sound was human, and it was coming from under a pile of fallen beams just inside the cabin.

''Who's there?'' David called as he moved cautiously through the gaping door frame and peered into the darkening shadows of the abandoned cabin. Splinters of lights came through holes in the roof, and as his eyes adjusted to the gloomy interior, he saw that the whole structure was ready to collapse. It wouldn't take much for the leaning wall joists to give way and bring the roof tumbling down.

He heard the whimper again, as he moved farther into the cabin. Then his breath caught. A woman's hand protruded from under a heap of tumbled boards.

''Paula?''

Chapter Twelve

As quickly and as carefully as David could, he began to move the smallest timbers off the pile. When he could see the dazed woman's face and the part of her body that wasn't pinned under the heaviest timbers, he knew she was barely conscious.

"Paula. Paula." He stroked her face and tried to rouse her, but a pitiful moan from her open mouth was her only response. "It's going to be all right. You hold on. I'm going after help." He cursed himself for leaving his cell phone in the Lexus.

As he turned away, his foot got tangled in some kind of strap. He picked it up and saw that it was attached to a camera. What on earth was Paula doing taking pictures in a place like this?

As fast as he could, he climbed back to the road where he'd left the Jeep. He couldn't believe how close he'd come to driving right by the spot. If he hadn't glanced in that direction when he had, he never would have seen the old cabin through the trees.

He drove at a mad speed back to the house, slamming on the brakes and bounding out of the car. He raced up the front steps and burst through the door, yelling, "I found her! I found her!"

Melissa and Carol were sitting in the living room reading a story to the children. They stared at him in shock and then jumped to their feet.

"You found Paula?"

"Where?"

"She's in that old cabin. About a half-mile down the road. I don't know how badly she'd hurt, but she's alive."

"Thank you, Lord." Melissa closed her eyes a moment in prayerful thanks.

"That's the old McGuire place," Carol said in disbelief. "I can't imagine why Paula would go there."

"She had a camera with her," David said as he grabbed up the telephone.

"Tell them they can reach the cabin from the dirt road along the river," Carol quickly told him as he dialed 911. "It will be faster."

As David made the call, Melissa and Carol hugged each other in prayerful joy. A moment ago they had been reading a scripture that promised "Call unto me, and I will answer." Melissa smiled to herself. Even though David would never admit it, in answer to their prayers he had been an instrument in God's hands.

"They're sending paramedics and alerting the search parties," David said as he hung up the phone.

"You go with him, Melissa," Carol said. "I'll watch the kids, and alert the men when they get back."

Melissa didn't argue. David reached out and grabbed her hand, and they raced out of the house together.

"Keep your eyes open for a glimpse of the cabin through those trees," he said as he headed the Jeep back the way he'd come. "I'm not exactly sure where it is. It was a miracle that I saw it at all."

Yes, a miracle, Melissa silently agreed.

Because they were going in the opposite direction, they weren't able to see down the hill clearly. They almost passed the place where David had left the road and hiked down to the cabin.

"I think this is it," he said, and made a sharp U-turn in the road to park the car. "Yes, there it is."

Melissa strained to see where he was pointing. The logs of the weathered cabin blended in so completely with the wooded hillside that it was incredible he had even noticed it. Just thinking that Paula had been lying there for almost three days made Melissa shiver.

They bounded out of the car and scrambled down the hillside, slipping and sliding on rocks and loose dirt and pushing through thick wild undergrowth. Melissa couldn't believe her eyes when they got close to the cabin; she was completely unprepared for its dilapidated condition. Half of the roof had already fallen in, and the rest of the building looked as if a strong wind would easily flatten it.

"What on earth was she doing here?" Melissa asked.

"She must have been taking pictures when she got trapped by some falling timbers."

Cautiously, they eased step by step into the darkened cabin. David had warned her not to touch any of the sagging walls. The boards under their feet creaked a warning as they put their combined weight on them, and Melissa held her breath that they wouldn't give way.

"She's over there." David pointed to the heap of fallen timbers that had been too heavy for him to move. He listened for a whimpering sound, but deadly silence met his ears. "Paula. Paula, we're here," he said, as they knelt down beside her.

Melissa swallowed hard, horrified by what Paula must be going through. How could anyone survive this long, trapped under the weight of those collapsed boards? As Melissa put her fingertips on the wrist of the hand lying free of the boards, she felt a faint pulse. Paula was still alive.

Almost immediately the shrill sound of a siren alerted them that the ambulance was coming up on a river road below the cabin. Melissa stayed with Paula, and David hurried out to explain everything to the two young male paramedics and their older driver.

"She's trapped inside under some fallen rafters," David told them. "And there's danger that the rest of the roof could go anytime."

The paramedics ordered Melissa out of the cabin, and quickly and efficiently assessed the situation. One of them admitted, "We can't do much for her until we can examine her and see what condition she's in. We'll have to radio for more help."

"The four of us should be able to move all the heavy timbers," David argued. "Why wait?"

"It could be risky," warned the driver. "What do you think, Smithy?" he asked the other man.

He thought a minute and then said, "If this here fellow's willing to give it a try, I say let's do it." He turned to the driver. "Call it in. We may need some backup help."

Melissa stood by, helpless, as the men disappeared inside the cabin. She could hear voices, and the scraping and shifting of boards. Her ears strained to hear any signs that the listing roof and walls were about to cave in on the men. She drew on her faith that God would not have brought them this far without his protection.

When the paramedics appeared for the stretcher that they had left outside, she knew they had successfully freed Paula. They were ready to bring her out! Tears of relief flowed down her cheeks as she waited, for what seemed like an eternity.

They finally appeared with Paula on the stretcher, covered with blankets and motionless. Melissa wished there was something she could do or say, but she had to be content just watching the men load her listless body into the ambulance. A minute later the doors slammed shut, and the ambulance was gone with the sound of the wailing siren.

When David turned to her, his face smudged with dirt and his hands scratched and bruised, she was so overcome with emotion that she couldn't speak. He had willingly jeopardized his life to save a woman he didn't even know. God's goodness ran through him, deep and true.

Why couldn't he see that there might be a greater

purpose to life than following a path that the world put before him?

When Melissa and David arrived at the modern, sixty-bed hospital, Paula was still in the emergency room. They were told that her condition was stable and she was undergoing a battery of tests to determine the extent of her injuries.

While they waited, they went to a small chapel, and Melissa knelt and prayed while David sat in the pew beside her. He closed his eyes and let a quiet peace flow through him.

The adrenaline rush of the rescue had taken its toll. He felt as if he'd been running full speed. He'd used every ounce of energy to get Paula safely out of the cabin before it totally collapsed. Every time they had removed a piece of timber, the whole structure vibrated. At the time he hadn't thought so much about his own life being in danger. He'd been worried that Paula might be closer to dying with every strangled breath.

He lowered his head and covered his eyes with his hands. Was Melissa right? The idea of his being a tool of a God in whom he really didn't believe was ludicrous and a little scary. He couldn't deny that this whole trip had been one of contradictions. His plans for a quick, easy trip to Wolfton and back had been thwarted at every turn. Would all this happen without design? The question made him uncomfortable. He had been drawn into a family unit with Melissa and the boys that he had never expected, and, in truth, didn't know how to handle. He'd never been this close to anyone, not even his own parents. If he didn't get back to Denver soon, he would lose his perspective and do something extremely foolish...like admitting that he had fallen in love with her. She'd made it clear what kind of husband and life she wanted. Even if he asked her to marry him, she'd never accept—despite the fact that marrying him would provide the home she wanted for Eric and Richie.

When she eased back on the seat, light coming through a stained-glass skylight bathed her face in a luminous light. She smiled at him and squeezed his hand. He had never seen a woman so beautiful. All lines of worry were gone from her face, as if she'd received a message of reassurance and peace.

When they returned to the E.R., they were given the good news. Paula had suffered no internal injuries. Only one rib was cracked and one bone broken in her right leg. She was suffering from shock and dehydration, but was already responding to treatment.

"No visitors for the time being," the doctor told them. "She needs rest for a day or two. Paula's one fortunate lady. From what the paramedics said, any one of those heavy timbers could have crushed her."

They were just about to leave the hospital, when Jim arrived breathless and anxious with Nancy. "We got here as fast as we could when we heard the news. How is she? Is she seriously hurt? What was she doing in a place like that?"

Nancy laid a soothing hand on his arm. "Easy, honey. Get hold of yourself."

He nodded. "Sorry. I just can't believe all of this."

David and Melissa tried to answer the flood of questions in a calm manner. Obviously Jim cared deeply for Paula and so did Nancy. They seemed like a caring couple who would have done anything for Paula.

When Melissa and David got back to the house, they were engulfed by a jubilant crowd of returning searchers.

"Hooray. Hooray for the man of the hour!" The men clapped David on the back.

Zach gave him a bear hug that almost squeezed the breath out of him. "Thank you, thank you. We'll never forget what you did this day." Tears filled the honorable judge's eyes as he hurried from the house and headed for the hospital, determined to see Paula even though he knew no visitors were allowed.

The sheriff shook David's hand. "Good man. I heard you risked your neck getting her out. You're made of good stuff. We're mighty grateful."

Even Mr. Shornberger was complimentary about David's success in finding the missing woman. There was just a tinge of surprise in his tone. Obviously, he had given David the chore of checking out the neighbors, thinking he wouldn't turn up much information.

Melissa could tell that David was embarrassed by all the fuss they were making over him. He seemed almost stunned by this outpouring of goodwill. She left him to enjoy his popularity and went in the kitchen to help Carol.

A half-dozen women crowded in the kitchen, busily setting out food and drink on the deck. Paula's picnic table was loaded down, and Eric, Richie and the Carlson girls were already sitting on the deck steps enjoying their full plates.

Carol hugged her. "Praise God."

"Amen," Melissa breathed, and they just held each other for a moment. Then the women began crowding around Melissa, introducing themselves. Their names escaped her but their warm smiles and kind words were a genuine welcome.

Everyone seemed to know that she'd brought Paula's nephews to visit, but nothing was said about the possibility of her keeping them. Apparently Paula had meant it when she refused to consider the responsibility of raising them. Now there seemed little hope that their visit would persuade Paula otherwise, but Melissa pushed away such thoughts. This was a time for thanksgiving. The lost had been found.

As each group of searchers returned to the house, the celebration swung into a greater expression of joy and gratitude. There were songs, laughter and prayers of thanksgiving. Neither David nor Melissa had experienced anything like it. The crowd kept getting bigger and bigger, spilling out into the yard as cars arrived with more of Paula's friends.

Melissa kept her eyes on the boys and made sure that Scruffy stayed close through all the comings and goings. Jim and Nancy returned to the house, and Melissa was pleased to see that they were reassured by their trip to the hospital. They shared with everyone what the doctor had said about Paula's condition.

The sun had set and most of the food was gone by the time people began to drift away with promises to keep in touch. Finally, when the Carlsons were the

only family left, David and Melissa began to realize
how exhausted they were. They had been caught in a
roller coaster of emotions since early morning.

"We'd love to have you come to church with us
in the morning, and stay for Sunday dinner, too."
Skip invited them with a nodding agreement from his
wife.

"Sunday?" Melissa said blankly. "Tomorrow's
Sunday?" She gave an embarrassed laugh. "I guess
I've lost track of the days."

Both Carol and Skip looked a little surprised. In
their world, Sunday was never forgotten.

"We were delayed getting here," David said without going into any further explanation. He wasn't
proud of the way he'd stubbornly headed into the
sandstorm with nearly tragic results. "I had planned
on being back in Denver two days ago."

"What a blessing that you weren't," Skip said solemnly. "You certainly were in the right place at the
right time, as far as we're concerned."

"I'm glad that things turned out the way they did,"
he admitted. "But I'm afraid I have no choice but to
head back as early in the morning as I can get away.
It's important that I get back to Denver as soon as
possible."

"But you and the boys will be staying on, won't
you, Melissa?" Carol asked. "I know Paula would
be brokenhearted if she missed your visit. Besides, it
would be a blessing to have someone in the house
with Paula when she comes home. She's an independent soul, but this ordeal is bound to take a lot out
of her."

"Our plans were for me to remain with the boys until Paula had a chance to get acquainted with them," Melissa answered easily. "I've made arrangements to send in my magazine articles from here."

"Good, I know Paula will be eager to tell you stories about her grandmother that you may be able to use." Carol laughed. "See how wonderfully bad things can be turned into good for everyone?"

Melissa tried to respond in an upbeat fashion, but the fact that David would be leaving in the morning sent her spirits in a downhill slide. She knew it was foolish to think that anything had changed. In spite of all the time they'd spent together, and the closeness that had been developing between them, he was still the same goal-oriented, success-driven man he'd always been.

After the Carlsons left, Melissa had little to say to him. She wanted to grumble that the state of Colorado ought to be able to do without him for a couple more days without falling off the face of the earth. Why couldn't he take charge of his life for once, and quit being a puppet on a political string? She knew she was being childish and selfish, but she didn't care. Her feelings for him had grown beyond a superficial friendship. It wasn't his fault, it was hers, but that didn't help her deal with the emptiness he'd leave behind.

When he offered to help put the boys down for the night, she refused. "Thanks, but you'd better get your own self to bed. Morning comes early. You won't want to waste any time getting on the road. You won't have us along to hold you back. You can drive as long and fast as you like.''

Her crisp tone startled him. ''I have to go, Melissa,'' he said apologetically. ''Please understand.''

''Oh, I understand. The governor's office would collapse if you were away another day or two.''

He saw her lip quiver and he said gently, ''It's not the governor's office I'm worried about. It's my career. If I'm not there to fulfill an important assignment, they'll give it to someone else. I can't afford to turn my back on opportunities that may not come again.''

''No, of course not.''

He sighed. ''I thought you realized how important my work is to me.''

''I guess I forgot. It's a good thing you reminded me.''

''Melissa—'' He reached out to her, but she turned away into Eric and Richie's bedroom. She heard him go into his room and shut the door. There was a finality about it that brought an ache to her heart.

She tried to hide her sinking spirits as she put the boys to bed, heard their prayers and tucked them in.

Eric wasn't fooled. ''Aren't you glad David found Aunt Paula?''

''Of course I'm glad. Why do you ask that?''

''Because your eyes don't smile anymore.''

''Maybe she's mad at us,'' Richie volunteered. ''We beat those girls real good in every game.'' An overtone of pride canceled out his concern that they'd done the wrong thing.

"Maybe they were just being nice and let you win," Melissa suggested with a smile.

Richie frowned. "Why would they do that?"

"Sometimes it's better to make other people happy, even if you have to lose to do it."

"Nobody likes to lose," Eric said.

"No, I guess not, but there's joy in doing the right thing, even if it's hard sometimes. I'm glad you had a good time and made some new friends." She hesitated, then said, "David will be going back to Denver in the morning, but we're staying here for a little while."

"Why can't he stay, too?" Eric frowned. "I thought he liked us." The slight quiver in his voice revealed a frightened little boy who had lost too many people in his young life.

Melissa hugged him. "Of course he likes you, but he has to get back to Denver. He has an important job and lots of people depend upon him."

"He bought us boots and everything," Richie said, as if that were reason enough for David not to go.

"Maybe we ought to go back, too?" Eric's eyes suddenly took on a hopeful shine. "Scruffy likes Denver better—don't you, Scruffy?"

The dog was stretched out on the foot of the bed, and at the sound of his name, he lifted his head and gave a responding "Woof."

"See!" Eric said. "He wants to go home, too."

Home? Not for a minute had she intended for the boys to consider David Ardell's house as *home*. She felt as if someone had landed a fist in her stomach. *Dear Lord, what have I done?*

Melissa tried to recover as best she could by changing the subject and talking about what a wonderful visit they were going to have staying here with Aunt Paula and all her friends.

When she left the bedroom, she went into her room and sat on the bed, staring at the floor. She'd never been one to lie to herself and she couldn't do that now. No man had ever created such an agonizing need in her to be a part of his life as David.

Surely, true love couldn't come like this.

She couldn't fall in love with a man whose goals in life would always be at odds with her deepest convictions. Why had God brought him into her life? Was the Lord testing her? Where was the deep sense of divine guidance that had always been her assurance?

Reaching for her Bible, she read Jeremiah 29:11: "For I know the plans I have for you, says the Lord, plans for good and not for evil, to give you a future and a hope." When she closed the book, she felt a sense of peace returning. *Let go. Let God.*

Early the next morning, when she heard David loading the car for his departure, she drew in a deep breath and lifted her chin. Then she went downstairs and waited for him to come back into the house after putting his suitcases in the Lexus.

When he saw her waiting for him in the living room, a frown flickered across his face, and as he walked toward her he seemed to brace his shoulders for another sharp rebuke about his leaving.

"I'm sorry," she said quickly, looking him squarely in the eyes. "I shouldn't have spoken to you the way I did. I was wrong. Of course you have to honor your commitments. I guess I was feeling off balance from everything that has happened.''

"I know. You don't have to apologize," he said, obviously relieved. "I'm just terribly sorry that I can't stay until things get settled."

"The boys and I will be fine here, really. Hopefully things will work out for Paula to keep the boys. If not, something else will. I have the feeling that this is a better place to find them a home than Denver, and I'll stay as long as I need to in order to get them settled."

"And what about you, and your writing?"

"I may have found a golden lode," she said, and quickly explained about Paula's grandmother. "So everything is working out well."

He reached out and let one finger play with a wayward curl falling on her cheek. "Is it?" His searching and questioning gaze was filled with a sudden longing. "I'm not so sure."

She fought against yielding to his touch, as he let his hands slip down to rest on her waist. She knew this was no time to give in to the deep feelings that he created in her. The moment he returned to Denver, he would be swept up in his frantic world and their paths would not cross again. Even as she told herself that she should purposefully walk away, she lifted her lips to meet his and leaned into his embrace.

He had kissed her lightly several times before, with a brush of his lips against her cheek or forehead, but this kiss was like the one that had sent her emotions reeling. There was a heat to his mouth pressed against hers. His hands molded the soft curves of her back, soothing and caressing.

"We can't let this go," he whispered. He didn't know how it had happened, but he'd found the woman he wanted. She was lovely, intelligent, gentle and loving. "This is so right…so right. You can't deny it."

She turned her head to avoid the warm, demanding pressure of his kisses and said breathlessly, "No, no it isn't right. It's wrong. All wrong."

"What is so wrong with us being in love? I want to marry you and build a life together."

She swallowed hard. "There's something very special between us, David, but it's not a foundation for marriage."

"Why not? We could keep the boys and start a family of our own. I'd learn to be a pretty good father, given a chance. And I'll make you proud of me. You might even end up as the First Lady of Colorado someday."

He said it with such pride that she wanted to cry. Didn't he realize that he had used the very argument that made any commitment to him impossible? Married to him, she would have to live in a political fishbowl. Her life would never be her own. She'd spend her time constantly trying to meet social demands and compromising her own integrity so she wouldn't embarrass him.

"I can't marry you, David."

"You don't have to give me an answer now," he said, as if she had just hesitated instead of giving him a flat rejection. "We'll keep in close touch by phone while you're here, and we can talk things out."

"There's nothing to talk out."

Her bluntness brought a flash of color to his cheeks. "You don't even want to think about it?"

"I have been thinking about it," she admitted. If he only knew how many hours she had agonized over the growing feelings she had for him. "I'm afraid my decision is final."

"I see. Well, I guess that settles that." He tried for a light laugh but failed. "I'd forgotten how stubborn you can be."

"David, you're a wonderful person and I don't know why God brought you into my life, but I'll be forever grateful. You'll always be very special to me."

"But not special enough to marry, I gather."

"I'm not the one for you, David," she said kindly, even as she felt a growing ache in her heart. She believed she was being sensible to voice her deep feelings now. He'd already been deeply hurt by one woman, and she couldn't bear to do that to him again. "I could never handle the pressures that go along with the kind of lifestyle you've chosen. In a way, you're already married to your career. Neither of us would be happy with the kind of compromises both of us would have to make."

"I'm sorry you feel that way." He'd never felt so much like a loser in his whole life, but he knew that further argument was useless. He cupped her sweet chin with his hand and allowed himself another brief kiss on her warm lips, before he turned away, firming a resolution to accept her rejection and put her out of his life and thoughts.

Chapter Thirteen

When Carol came by to pick up Melissa and the boys for Sunday School and church, she poked her head in the door and called, "Anybody home?"

"We're almost ready," Melissa called back as she came out of the kitchen. "The boys are finishing up their breakfast."

Although she knew she was in need of some spiritual recharging, Melissa wished she could just hide out for the day. She didn't feel like facing a bunch of new people.

Carol took one look at her listless expression and said, "Let me guess. David left?"

Melissa nodded. "About four o'clock. He likes to get an early start when he's traveling." An unbidden memory of their early morning walk by the river threatened a wash of emotion that she struggled to hide. "I wouldn't be surprised if he drove straight through to Denver."

"And you wish you'd gone with him?" Carol asked.

Melissa shook her head. "No, my place is here for the moment."

"You don't look very happy about it," Carol commented with her usual frankness. "If I didn't know better I'd guess that you two had a fight. I know it's none of my business, but if you need an ear, I'm your gal."

Melissa was used to handling problems on her own, and she'd never had a really close friend, someone to share things that were bothering her. She couldn't believe it when she heard herself saying, "David asked me to marry him, and I turned him down."

"I see. And you're having second thoughts?" Carol asked with a concerned frown.

"No. I made the right decision," Melissa said firmly. She had gone over all the things they had said to each other. Even if she'd taken time to think about his proposal as he suggested, she would have refused. It wouldn't be fair to him or to her to settle for a marriage that wasn't supportive for either of them.

"You don't love him?" Carol asked with an edge of skepticism.

Melissa managed a weak smile. "I love him so much, I feel as if someone has planted a dagger in my chest."

"Then, why…"

As succinctly as she could, Melissa tried to explain the situation to Carol.

Carol took her hand and squeezed it. "Sometimes we don't see how the sun is ever going to come out and shine again, but it always does. There's a rhythm to God's blessings if we'll just keep the faith and let the good times roll around again.'' She grinned. ''How about that for a good affirmation to start every day? Let the good times roll. After all, the Lord promised blessings pressed down and overflowing.''

The way Carol mixed the Holy with the vernacular was delightful. How could anyone be despondent when she was around? Melissa chuckled. ''Let the good times roll.''

''I think we're kindred spirits,'' Carol said, winking at her.

Melissa felt at home almost immediately in the small, simple sanctuary with stained-glass windows depicting Bible stories, and wooden pews polished to a golden hue. It was exactly the kind of church her grandmother would have loved.

Skip Carlson looked strange to her in his clerical robe and polished black shoes. In her mind's eye, she kept seeing him as he was dressed yesterday, in faded blue jeans, western shirt and boots. Carol boldly winked at him when she caught his eye. He seemed perfectly at ease behind the lectern, and spoke in an easy, personal way that made his sermon seemed like a friendly chat with each member of the congregation. Melissa silently added her own petitions for understanding and a willingness to accept the future as it unfolded.

After church the sincere concern some of the parishioners extended to Melissa eased some of the discomfort she felt, living in a strange house, in unfamiliar surroundings and waiting for a woman whom she'd never met to come home. She refused all the invitations except the one from Skip.

"You'll come to our house for Sunday dinner, won't you?" the minister asked as he stood at the door, shaking hands after the service. "Carol put in a roast this morning with plenty of vegetables, and I spied a couple of apple pies that she made last night."

Melissa accepted without hesitation. "And thanks for the message this morning. I needed to be reminded about keeping an 'attitude of gratitude.'"

"We all tend to forget what we already have, and dwell on what we want," he agreed.

"Not me," Carol said, overhearing his words as she joined them with the children. "When I forget to count my blessings, Skip reminds me. Don't you, honey?" she teased.

He grinned at her, and Melissa saw a tender look of love pass between them. "Just doing my job."

Carol slipped her arm through his. "Come on, Preacher, let's go home."

The afternoon spent at their house was a healing one for Melissa. The Carlson home celebrated a joyful acceptance of the Lord's presence and constant blessing. Peace radiated in the midst of normal family chaos. It reinforced her determination to hold out for the kind of marriage and family life she wanted.

David had been on the road nearly eighteen hours when he finally checked into a motel. The long drive across Wyoming had been filled with constant reminders of Melissa and the boys. He tried to close his mind to memories that were only a mockery, in light of the way the whole business had ended. How in the world had he allowed himself to get into this fiasco in the first place?

He went over in his mind everything that had happened. He had just wanted to honor Jolene's wishes, and each step of the way seemed innocent enough. How could he have known that he was going to fall head over heels in love with a woman who despised everything that was important in his life? And how had two kids and an ugly dog gotten under his skin the way they had?

He glanced at his watch. Six o'clock. The kids' suppertime. No doubt, Melissa would have plenty of offers to eat out. He thought about the celebration gathering, and all the friendly people who had brought food and drink. He was sure they'd look after her and the boys. They'd be fine.

He stared at the bedside phone. It wouldn't hurt to check. Before he could change his mind, he found Paula's number and called the house. After four rings, the answering machine clicked on and he listened to Melissa's sweet voice on the recorded message.

She sounded confident and upbeat.

Slowly he replaced the receiver without leaving a message, chiding himself for thinking she might feel as empty on the inside as he did.

Melissa checked the answering machine when she came in from the boys' picnic. There were two calls, from a neighbor and from someone else who had not left a message. The phone rang several times during the evening and each time she held her breath, hoping to hear David's strong resonant voice—but it was always one of Paula's well-wishers.

Well, what did she expect, she asked herself as she dealt with the disappointment. The truth was, there was little more to be said between them. He was as strong-willed as she was, and there was little ground for compromise. She wouldn't give up her strong Christian family values. The only bond between them was the welfare of the boys. Once they were placed, she'd probably never see the illustrious David Ardell, except in the newspapers or on TV.

That night she read her Bible, said her prayers and went to sleep on a tear-stained pillow.

Carol and Skip brought Paula home two days later. Melissa and the boys were on the front porch waiting to greet her as the car drove up.

Paula's hazel eyes were bright and clear as she stepped out of the car with Skip's help. One arm was in a cast, and she moved gingerly, but her full mouth spread in a welcoming grin when she saw the welcoming party coming down the steps toward her. She was a small woman, about four feet eleven inches tall. Her face was round, framed by brown hair cut short for easy care.

"Well, here I am. You must think I have a screw loose," she said, smiling and looking slightly embarrassed. "I was wanting to make an impression—and I guess I did."

"Always going for the dramatic," Carol teased. "You really outdid yourself this time, sweetheart."

"Let's not have any encores." Skip grinned fondly
at her. "It's time you met these two handsome nephews of yours." He motioned for the boys to come
closer, and he playfully ruffled their hair as he introduced them. "This is Eric. He's six years old and has
a lot of smart questions popping around in that head
of his. And this bright fellow is Richie, and he has
more energy than a pack of monkeys."

"I'm very happy to meet you both," Paula said
warmly. "I'm very glad you came to see me." She
didn't rush at them with any hugs and kisses, but
Melissa thought she caught a glimpse of moisture in
Paula's eyes as she looked at them.

"And this is Melissa," Carol said, pulling her forward.

"You're as pretty in person as you sounded on the
phone. I'm sorry about the delayed welcome."

Impulsively Melissa kissed her cheek. "This is the
best welcome we could have."

"What were you doing poking around in the old
cabin, anyway? I would have thought you had better
sense than that," Skip chided her with affection.

Paula answered with spirit. "While I was waiting
for the boys to arrive, I thought I'd walk down to the
river and take a few photos. On the way down the
hill, I saw this prissy mother raccoon with four dar-
ling little ones just outside the cabin. I thought they
would make some cute pictures to show the boys, so
when they disappeared into the cabin, I decided to
slip inside and snap a few. I guess just the weight of
my body caused something to shift. All of a sudden,
the whole place seemed to be falling down on me."

Her voice wavered, and Carol quickly put an arm around Paula's waist. "You are home, and that's all that matters."

Once inside the house, Paula looked around slowly as if she had never expected to see it again. Obviously, all those hours of being helplessly trapped had left their mark, and Melissa knew that Paula would need some emotional healing along with the physical.

Carol and Skip were wonderful with Paula, and Melissa and the boys stayed in the background as they settled her on the living room sofa.

When the boys brought Scruffy inside, Melissa held her breath. Obviously the verdict was still out on the boys' acceptance of Aunt Paula, pending her attitude toward the dog. It was obvious, in their childish reasoning, that if Scruffy wasn't welcome, neither were they. Wagging his scrawny tail, he greeted Carol and Skip and then danced over to the sofa to sniff at the newcomer, while Eric and his brother told her about Scruffy's escapades.

Melissa's spirits took wing as she looked at the boys' grinning faces and the tenderness in Paula's eyes. A bond of affection was already evident between them, and Melissa began to relax. It was going to be all right.

The next few days just about convinced Melissa that they'd found the perfect place for the boys. Even with her injuries, Paula was not content to sit idly by and twiddle her thumbs. She had shoeboxes full of pictures that she'd taken of deer, elk and about every other animal that had ever shown up on the mountains around Wolfton.

"How about making some nice posters?" she asked the boys. "You can paste the pictures you like on a large piece of cardboard and hang them on the wall in your room."

"Neat." She had shown Eric a bunch of horse pictures, and he was all for it.

Richie decided on bears for his poster. He was still a little disgruntled that they hadn't seen any in Yellowstone.

While Melissa took care of house chores and smiled secretly to herself, Paula entertained the boys with stories of her childhood growing up in this mountain valley. More and more, Melissa became convinced that once Paula recovered physically from her ordeal, she might be reluctant to turn down the chance to keep them. She was almost positive that Paula would not want Eric and Richie to be turned over to strangers to raise. But forcing her too soon into making a decision about keeping the boys was not a good idea. Although she was eager to talk about the boys' future, she forced herself to be patient.

She waited for a couple of days before mentioning her own interest in Paula's family and background. When she told her that she was collecting material for a book about courageous pioneer women of faith, Paula's eyes sparkled. "Let me tell you about my great-grandmother."

"Please do," Melissa said eagerly, and then confessed that Carol had already mentioned Paula's grandmother as a perfect subject for her book. "I can't help but believe that the Lord brought me here so that I can tell her story."

Melissa was completely overwhelmed by the wealth of material that Paula shared with her: journals, old photographs and personal accounts of this courageous lady who had ridden horseback through all kinds of weather, night and day, to nurse the sick.

"That's her Bible," Paula said, pointing to a weathered, leather-bound volume lying on a nearby shelf. "She always took it in the saddlebag with her. Sometimes when I open it, I can almost hear her sweet voice reading me some of her favorite passages."

Melissa listened attentively, as Paula shared wonderful stories that had been handed down by families in the valley who had experienced her great-grandmother's unselfish dedication.

Paula's eyes misted when she said, "I'm so proud that you are going to tell her story."

Paula had quite a few people dropping in to see her, but Judge Daniels was the most frequent visitor. Melissa tried to make sure the boys didn't raise any ruckus while he was there, but after a couple of visits she began to relax. He was more than cordial to her and insisted that she call him Zach, instead of Judge.

"That's a fine young man of yours," he told her. "He showed lots of courage and foresight. I bet he's a darn good lawyer."

"The governor of Colorado thinks so," Melissa said, agreeing with his last statement and ignoring his implication that David was her young man. "David is his legal counsel."

"Is that right?" The judge looked duly impressed

before he sauntered outside. They could hear him laughing with Eric and Richie as they played catch.

"He's good with kids," Paula said with an approving nod.

When Melissa teased Paula about his attentions, she just smiled sheepishly. "It's kinda nice having him around."

"Why haven't you ever married him?"

"You know, while I was lying there, almost dead, I kept asking myself the same question. I just may say yes, the next time he asks me."

Melissa hoped Paula didn't see the leap of joy that surged through her. Paula and Zach! Perfect. The boys would have a wonderful male role model and the tender care of an aunt who loved them.

Although Paula fussed about having to go to the doctor for a checkup after a week had passed, Melissa left the boys with Carol and drove her there in the Jeep.

While she was having an X ray made, the doctor asked Melissa if she'd be staying with Paula for an extended time.

Melissa explained that she had brought Paula's nephews for a visit. "We're hoping that she will be willing to give them a home," she added.

"You mean, take them to raise?" he asked sharply. When she nodded, he shook his head. "No, that's impossible."

Melissa's mouth went dry. "Why?"

"Paula's medical condition is such that she needs to cut back on her activities, not take on the responsibility of raising two young boys. She didn't agree to keep them, did she?''

"No," Melissa said, her chest suddenly tight. "We just thought that—"

"Well, you thought wrong." The doctor leveled stern eyes on her. "It's a miracle this last fiasco of hers didn't kill her. Paula is one brave lady, but I don't think even she would be foolish enough to consider taking on the responsibility of an adopted family." He gave Melissa a warning look. "Paula has a medical condition that is under control but could be exacerbated by stress. You'll have to find someone else to raise those boys."

Chapter Fourteen

David returned to the office, worn out from the hard drive from Montana, and instantly was caught up in a never-ending maze of demands. He couldn't believe the backlog of work waiting for his attention. The list of calls to be returned looked like a telephone directory. He'd never felt so swamped by work in his life, or less like doing any of it.

His secretary eyed him frankly. "Your little vacation certainly didn't do you a lot of good."

"It wasn't a vacation," he responded shortly. "Personal business."

"Did you get rid of those kids who've been living at your house?" Elsie asked, ignoring the "no trespassing" tone of his voice.

"We think we've found a place for Eric and Richie," he answered without elaborating. He wasn't about to grease the gossip mill with any comments about his trip. At that moment, he was trying to sort out all the drama and trauma that had left his emotions in a muddle. His thoughts kept centering on what was happening with Melissa and the boys. How soon would she be coming back to Denver? Would she let him know? Probably not, he thought with painful resignation. She couldn't have been much clearer about not wanting him in her life.

"What about Ms. Chanley? Did she come back with you?" Elsie asked, as if reading his thoughts.

"No. She stayed," he said shortly, and then asked abruptly, "What meetings have been rescheduled?"

She gave him an updated calendar and suggested that he call Stella Day for confirmation. He did so.

"So you're back," Stella said in a relieved voice. When she had told him that the governor had held the important committee appointment open for him, he breathed a sigh of relief.

"You're one lucky guy," she told him. "There are a half-dozen guys who would kill to be on that committee. A word of warning, though. I don't think the governor will go for any more disappearing acts. I'd stay pretty close to home if I were you."

"Don't worry, I'm not going anywhere," he reassured her.

"There's a reception at the governor's mansion this weekend. Better send your tux out to the cleaners and get your hair trimmed."

"Yes, Mother," he mocked. "Anything else?"

"Don't get derailed, David, or you'll get left at the political starting gate."

He had little time to think about anything but fulfilling his obligations, as he prepared reports, met with the governor's staff and attended a marathon of meetings. Even after spending ten to twelve hours at the office, he brought work home with him. Sometimes he didn't turn off the light in his den until after midnight, but even then the house closed in on him with its emptiness.

Sometimes he wandered into the kitchen, tired but not wanting to go to bed. When he saw Scruffy's water dish still sitting on the floor, he suppressed a peculiar wrench in the pit of his stomach. He'd never been one to be sentimental or nostalgic about things or people, but the kitchen echoed with the memory of the children's loud voices and Melissa's laughter, and he felt a poignant sense of loss.

He wasn't the only one who found the house much too empty and quiet. Both Inga and Hans had bombarded him with questions about the boys, and Paula's rescue. He left out the drama of his part in the rescue, and simply said they found her in an old cabin with some minor injuries. "I'm sure she's back home now, enjoying Melissa and the boys."

"You don't know for sure?" Inga asked with her usual directness. "They don't have telephones in Montana?"

"I called once. Melissa said everything was fine," he hedged. He'd been tempted a hundred times since he'd been back to pick up the phone and call her, but usually the impulse came at an inopportune moment at work or late at night. And what was there to say? *I miss you. I love you. Why won't you marry me?* He knew that nothing he said was going to change her mind. Melissa had been right about their not being suited to each other.

"You call." Inga shook her finger in a scolding fashion. "I'm not blind. I saw what was happening when Melissa and the boys were here. You were happy and smiling and enjoying yourself. Now you are the same old David, buried in work."

Daniel smiled at her motherly chastising. All the time he was growing up, it was Inga that he ran to with his problems, not his mother. "All right. You win. I'll call her tomorrow."

"Good. And you tell her that we *all* miss her."

Melissa and Paula were out on the deck with the boys having lunch, when the telephone rang.

"Let the machine pick it up," Paula said. "I don't feel like shooting the breeze with anyone right now."

"It might be Carol. I thought I might run over and see her and Skip this evening," Melissa said.

"Well, you better answer it, then. I'm so glad the two of you have struck up a friendship."

"Me, too. I've never had a real close girlfriend before," Melissa said as she pushed back her chair and hurried into the house. She grabbed the phone on the last ring. When she heard David's voice responding to her hurried, "Hello," she caught her breath.

"You sound out of breath," he said lightly. "What's happening?"

It took Melissa a second to handle the surprise, and the sudden joy that shot through her. "I was out on the deck and ran inside to catch the phone before the answering machine clicked on."

"That's what I got when I called before."

"But...you didn't leave a message."

"No, I just wanted to know if everything was all right, and your recording said, 'All is well,' so I didn't want to bother you."

His silence had bothered her more than a dozen calls would have. For the first few days, every time the phone rang, she leaped at it. Then she took hold of herself. *Quit being a lovesick fool,* an inner voice had mocked. *Be realistic.* She'd read his silence, loud and clear. He was getting on with his life, and she would have to do the same.

"How are things going in Denver?" she asked evenly, her heart thumping around in her chest like an off-balance gyroscope.

"Hectic, as usual. It hasn't been easy getting back in the groove," he admitted. "How are things with you?"

Melissa hesitated. "I'm afraid things aren't going the way we had hoped."

"What's wrong?" His voice was suddenly filled with concern. "Are you and the boys all right?"

"We're fine. It's Paula, I'm afraid."

"Is she still in the hospital?" he asked anxiously.

"No, she's home and recovering nicely, but I had a startling talk with her doctor when I took her in for a checkup." She told him about what the doctor had said about Paula. "It's a miracle that she's still alive after what happened to her."

There was a heavy silence on his end. "Well, then, I guess we'd better bring them back to Denver and see what can be done from here."

"I think there's another possibility," she said quickly. "When we were at Carol's and Skip's for

Sunday dinner, it came to me that they would be a perfect couple to raise Eric and Richie. The boys get along great with their daughters. Skip is tender, caring and supportive, and it's obvious that he would enjoy being a father to two sons. It would be a wonderful Christian home for Eric and Richie.''

"Have you said anything to Skip and Carol about all of this?''

"Not yet. I've been waiting for the right time. I can't help but believe that there's some divine reason for us to have made the trip here, and if Paula can't give the boys a home, another one will be provided with God's blessing. You liked them, didn't you?''

"Yes, I did,'' he answered without hesitation. "And I think it would be great if they took the boys. Wolfton is a nice little town, and the people really seem to care about each other.'' He'd never forget the way people had gathered at Paula's house after she'd been found, hugging and laughing. He liked Skip's friendliness and sense of humor. "I wish I could be there to talk to them with you.''

"I wish you could, too. I don't suppose you could get away again anytime soon.''

"I'm afraid not,'' he said. "We'll have to figure something out when you're ready to come back to Denver. How long do you think you'll stay?''

"It depends. Even if Skip and Carol take the boys, I won't want to leave immediately. I've found some wonderful material for my book.'' Excitedly, she told him about Paula's great-grandmother. "Can you believe it? Her story is exactly what I've been looking for.''

He could picture her blue eyes shining and a smile lighting up her whole face as she talked. Just listening to her touched him in ways he hadn't thought possible. He'd been a fool to wait this long to call her.

She laughed. "Sorry, I didn't mean to bend your ear like that. It's just that I miss not having you here to share all these things with me."

"I miss being there. And I miss having you and the boys here in the house," he confessed. "It's just not the same."

"You mean it's too peaceful without all of Eric's and Richie's shenanigans?" she teased.

"You should hear the way Inga and Hans talk about you and the boys. They think it's my fault that you're not coming back. I was tempted to tell them that I'd proposed to you but you turned me down flat."

"Oh, David, please forgive me if I hurt you. It's just that…that…" She tried to find the right words.

"I know. You don't want to live your life in a three-ring circus. I guess I can't blame you. Sometimes I wonder why I do," he admitted frankly. "Anyway, you're right about one thing. Politically ambitious lawyers make poor husbands. You deserve better."

"And so do you, David." She was glad he couldn't see the tears filling her eyes. "I just couldn't be the kind of wife you want."

Yes, you could! he protested silently. *You're everything I want in a woman. Everything.* Aloud, he said, "I think we've been down this road before. Anyway, I just called to see how things were going, not to try to pressure you into changing your mind—although that's always an option open to you," he said as evenly as he could.

"I'll remember that," she said, disguising a sudden tightening in her chest.

"Well, then, we'll stay in touch. If you arrange something definite for the boys, let me know. And if you need anything at all, I'll get back to you right away. I promise." He almost asked her if he could speak to the boys, but decided against it. There really wasn't anything he could say to them that would help them understand the situation. They probably thought he'd deserted them, and David wasn't up to Eric's point-blank questioning.

After they said goodbye and Melissa hung up the receiver, she stared at it for a long time. Then she went into the bathroom to wash the tears off her face.

The affair at the governor's mansion was like many others that David had attended. A small, select group of guests mingled in first-floor rooms before dinner, while waiting for the governor and the first lady of Colorado to make their appearance from private quarters above.

When he felt a tug on the sleeve of his black jacket, he turned to find Pamela Wainwright smiling up at him. Stella had already alerted him that the senator's daughter was to be one of the guests.

"What was your name again?" she teased. "It's been so long since I've seen you, I've forgotten. Someone said you were in Montana."

"That's right," David responded easily, ignoring

the questioning in her tone. It was none of her business where he'd been and why. Only Elsie and Stella had known the reason for his absence.

"Stella said that you might like to tell me all about it over dinner."

"Really?" David kept a practiced smile on his face while he silently fumed. He was sick and tired of Stella trying to manipulate a romantic relationship between him and this social-climbing debutante. Pamela bored him, irritated him and set his teeth on edge with her superficial chatter.

"I rather suspect we'll find our dinner place cards next to each other," she added coyly, as if this were evidence of some kind of intimacy between them.

David silently groaned. If he had a chance, he'd slip into the dining room and switch the place cards. A little of Pamela's company went a long way. Unfortunately, she stayed at his side and hung on him in a way that let everyone in the gathering know that she considered David and her "a couple."

Even the beautifully served dinner couldn't rescue David from total boredom and frustration. He tried to make a good impression on important dignitaries who had been invited to the dinner because they had influence in state affairs, but he wasn't at his best. He was relieved when the evening ended and he could make his escape from the pressure of being politically correct in everything he said and did.

Melissa and the boys were invited to go with Carol and Skip to a potluck dinner at the church. Paula had been included in the invitation, but she said she'd rather go to bed early with a good book.

The church's community room was in the basement, and long tables filled most of the floor space between the kitchen and a small stage at the other end of the room.

"The men are going to serve the meal and the children have been working up skits and songs," Carol told her as they placed their dishes on an already loaded serving table.

"My Sunday School class is going to sing 'Jesus Loves Me,'" Holly said proudly.

"We know that one," Richie said with a broad grin. "Melissa taught it to us—didn't she, Eric?"

"Then, you can sing it with us."

"Can we?" Eric asked in surprise. Both boys shot a look at Melissa.

"Maybe we better ask Nancy. She's in charge of the program," Melissa said, nodding at Jim's wife, Nancy, who was sitting at the table with them. She was a young, sweet, caring woman who obviously loved children.

"Of course. That's a wonderful idea," Nancy agreed. "We could use two more boys in the children's choir."

As Melissa looked around the room, she saw that some of the men wearing aprons were the same ones who had been at Paula's house to help in the search. Skip waved to them from the kitchen, wearing a chef's hat that made him look seven feet tall. Zach and Jim hovered around their table, pouring coffee and lemonade.

"Have you heard from that hero of ours?" Jim asked. "We ought to give him a medal or something."

"He proved himself to be one courageous fellow," Zach agreed. "If it hadn't been for him, we could have lost my sweet Paula."

Melissa would have given anything if David could be there to see the sincere admiration on their faces. Whether he knew it or not, he had made some loyal friends.

"Too bad he couldn't stick around a while. He seems like a regular fellow, all right," Jim said. "He's got plenty of guts, I'll say that for him."

"People can't quit talking about the way he saved Paula," Zach agreed. "He's a hero."

Richie looked puzzled and popped up with "What's a hero?"

"Well, young fellow," Zach said, smiling down at the little boy, "a hero is somebody who risks his own life to save somebody else's. The way David saved your aunt Paula."

"Oh," Richie said thoughtfully.

"He saved our dog, too," Eric boasted.

Zach laughed. "Then, he's a hero two times over."

At that moment, Skip rang a dinner bell and waited until he had everyone's attention. When a hush had fallen on the room, he gave thanks for the food, fellowship and all of God's blessings. A murmur of "amens" was followed by a joyful announcement: "Let's eat!"

"This is wonderful," Melissa told Carol, as they filed through a buffet line with loaded plates and helped the children put something on theirs besides dessert.

"Why don't you stick around? You could work on your book here just as well as in Denver, couldn't you?" Carol asked.

"The reality is that it'll probably take me a year to get my book ready to market," Melissa explained. "And I may be offered an editor's job when I get back."

"Good for you. But you have to promise not to forget us when you and the boys get back to the big city. They're lucky to have someone like you looking after them. It's wonderful you took the time to bring them here to visit their aunt. They're sweet, adorable kids."

When Melissa saw the way Carol's eyes were shining as she looked at Eric and Richie seated next to her own little girls, Melissa decided the time had come to share the hope that had been building inside her. She watched how beautifully Eric and Richie fit into this wonderful Christian family, and she couldn't help but wonder if this could be the loving home that the Lord had planned for the boys all along.

She turned to Carol. "Could we excuse ourselves for a minute? I have something I want to talk to you about."

"Sure." Carol laid down her napkin. "We'll be back in a minute, kids. Don't leave the table."

She led the way upstairs to a small ladies' rest room, complete with vanity table and a couple of upholstered chairs. As soon as Carol closed the door, she raised a questioning eyebrow. "Have you heard from David?"

"Yes, but this isn't about him. It's about the boys." She told Carol everything about Jolene's note, and David's sense of duty to try to place the boys in a good home. She admitted that they'd brought them to visit Paula with the hope that she would grow so fond of them that she'd agree to keep them.

"But she's not physically able to raise two boys," Carol said.

"We know that, now. Of course, Paula keeping them is out of the question." Melissa took a deep breath and plunged ahead. "The truth is, we haven't been able to locate anyone else on either side of the family who could take them. They need someone to give them a loving home, and I've watched how beautifully you and Skip are raising your little girls..."

Carol's eyes widened as if she knew what was coming next. "What are you trying to say, Melissa?"

"Wouldn't you love adding two wonderful little boys to your family?"

Carol gave a surprised laugh. "You mean, you haven't noticed?" She patted her tummy. "I'm almost four months pregnant, and the doctor thinks it may be twins. I'm afraid our little house is already going to be bulging at the seams with these new arrivals."

"Oh, Carol, that's wonderful." Melissa was torn between being happy about Carol's news, and devastated by her own disappointment. How could she have been so wrong? She tried to keep her voice optimistic. "Of course you're going to have your hands

full. Obviously, my idea is not the answer I've been
praying for.''

''Sometimes we just have to wait on the Lord to
bring about our highest blessing,'' Carol said as she
hugged Melissa. ''Keep the faith.''

They went back to their table, and as Melissa
watched Eric and Richie standing on the stage happily
singing ''Jesus Loves Me'' slightly off-key with all
the other children, she felt estranged from God. Her
faith wavered the way Job's had when he thought the
Lord had deserted him. She felt alone, adrift, and
without hope.

That night, after putting the boys to bed, she went
downstairs and picked up the old Bible that had sus-
tained Paula's great-grandmother through so many
uncertain times. Before she had opened it, however,
the telephone rang.

She glanced at her watch. Ten o'clock. Who would
be calling this late? Then her heart lurched. Could it
be?

When she heard his voice, she cried happily, ''David, how nice of you to call.''

''I hope it's not too late. I just got home from a
miserable evening.''

''Mine wasn't the best,'' she admitted with a catch
in her voice.

''What happened? Honey, what's wrong?''

''Carol and Skip are going to have another baby,
maybe twins. They can't take Eric and Richie. I can't
believe it. It would have been perfect. I had it all
planned out.'' If he reminded her that she'd been
preaching to him ''Let go and let God,'' she'd hang

up on him. "It was the answer we've been looking
for," she stubbornly insisted.

"Apparently not," he said gently.

"You know, I'm beginning to think that I've been
looking at this in the wrong way."

"What do you mean?"

"Carol asked me tonight why I didn't stay in Wolfton, and I've been tossing the idea around. I'm pretty
sure Paula would let the boys and me live here while
I hunt for some kind of job. The people I've met have
been very kind and supportive, and I love Skip's
church. With that kind of support group, I think I
could adopt Eric and Richie and do right by them as
a single parent. What do you think?"

"What about your writing career?" he asked, not
wanting to come right out and say that it was an ir-
rational idea. "Don't you have a future there?"

"Yes, but it's not as important as the boys' future," she said in a tone that offered no room for
argument. "I'll let you know when I've decided."

"Melissa, you have your own life to think about
and—"

"Don't lecture me," she said shortly.

"I'm not lecturing you. I just don't think you
should make life-changing decisions on the basis of
emotion."

"What *should* you base them on? Hard, cold em-
pirical facts?" She knew she was being unfair, but
disappointment made her less than generous. "I'll let
you know what I've decided."

He couldn't believe how effectively she'd slammed

the door shut on him and any argument he might offer. When she told him goodbye, there was a finality
about it that left him gripping the phone so tightly
that his knuckles turned white.

Chapter Fifteen

Melissa didn't say anything to anyone as she began to quietly move forward in her plan to remain in Wolfton with the boys. She prayed and searched her heart, knowing that any sacrifice she made to raise the boys would be more than balanced by the happiness of watching them grow into strong Christian men.

But the job market was not a good one. The only opportunity that presented itself was an assistant's job at the public library. She knew she would love working there—but could she possibly manage on the low salary? She decided it was time to talk to Paula and share her plans.

They were sitting at the kitchen table enjoying a midday cup of coffee, while the boys and Scruffy played on the hill behind the house. Climbing and sliding, they scrambled through the trees in games of hide-and-seek. Melissa had never seen them so carefree and happy. Their squeals of laughter quickened her heart with happiness.

She put down her coffee cup and cleared her throat. Not knowing exactly how to begin, she searched for the right words, but before she could say anything, Paula dropped a surprise package of her own.

With a confidential smile, she leaned toward Melissa. "I want you to be the first to know. I've decided to marry Zachary. Can you believe it?"

Melissa had been so intent on telling Paula about her own plans that she was taken by surprise. She shouldn't have been. It was obvious how the judge felt about Paula. Melissa wondered if Paula ever would have said yes if it hadn't been for the accident. Somehow a near brush with death put things in a different perspective.

Melissa reached over and squeezed her hand. "I think that's wonderful."

"Zach's been asking me for ages, so it isn't anything sudden. We dated quite a lot a few years back, and he even rented a room from me once." Her eyes twinkled. "I think he's been ready to move back in ever since."

"I'm so happy for you," Melissa said sincerely. "You shouldn't live your life alone."

"That's what I decided. All those long hours, lying hurt in that cabin. I kept thinking about Zach and how sad he would be if I died. I don't know how many years I have left, but there are a lot of things we could do together. Having him around the house would be a joy. He's quite a cook, you know." She gave a girlish chuckle. "I'll probably put on ten pounds the first month."

"Have you set a date?"

"Not yet, but soon. We don't want to waste any more time. I hope you and the boys can stay long enough to see us tie the knot. It'll be nice to have some of my own family there."

"Of course we can," she said readily, even as her plans to remain at Paula's for an undetermined time collapsed. With Zach moving in, she and the boys would have to move out. With no job and no place to live, the door slammed shut on the possibility of staying in Wolfton. She shoved away the enveloping clouds of uncertainty and concentrated on Paula's happiness.

"Just tell me how I can help."

"I haven't thought much about the ceremony. I'll probably ask Nancy to be my matron of honor, and Jim can give me away. Both of them have been so good to me. All the time he lived in the house, he was like my son. When he married, Nancy became family, too."

Melissa nodded her approval. She remembered how distraught Jim had been that first day when he'd discovered Paula had not come home.

"We haven't decided about the honeymoon. Maybe Hawaii. I've always wanted to wade in those beautiful ocean waters." She laughed like a young girl. "There are a whole lot of dreams that will be coming true."

Just then, they heard the front door open, and Carol's merry "hello" floated through the house.

"Anybody home? I smell coffee and fresh-made muffins," she declared as she came into the kitchen with her usual energetic bounce. "May I join you, ladies? I've had breakfast, but I'm eating for two—or maybe three," she said, winking at Melissa.

Paula's eyes immediately traveled over Carol's roomy pullover. "Are you pregnant?"

"Guilty as charged," she laughed, and patted her rounding tummy.

As Melissa listened to Paula's and Carol's excited chatter, she struggled to come to terms with her own crumbling plans. She was glad she hadn't called and turned down the upcoming editor's job. She didn't know how in the world she would swing moving to a larger place, or absorb the expenses of raising two boys, but at the moment she could see no other path.

David was sitting at his desk reviewing his calendar for the day, when his secretary buzzed him. "Judge Daniels from Wolfton, Montana, is on the line."

Zachary. Why was he calling? David's first thought was that something had happened to Paula. "Hi, Judge. This is a surprise. Is everything all right?"

"Fine. I hope this is a good time to call. I know you're a busy man."

"No problem. Is something wrong?"

"Far from it." Zachary cackled. "I feel like a maverick turned loose in a meadow of green grass. I'm getting married. Paula and I are tying the knot. How about that?"

David laughed in relief. "Congratulations. That's great. When's the happy day?"

"Haven't decided. I've got some things to get set-tled first, and I've got a proposition for you. I don't want any 'no' answer until you've considered it."

"What kind of a proposition?"

"It's like this. I've been a district judge for the past fifteen years and I'm ready to get off the bench. I'm resigning, and I'm opening up my old law office. I've been making some enquiries about you. Your legal career is impressive, David. For a man your age, your experience is outstanding. You've got a reputation for being a top-notch lawyer, and keeping your head on straight when things get tough. I want to make you an offer. How does a full partnership in my law firm sound to you?"

"Are you serious?"

"Absolutely. What do you say?"

"I'll have to get back to you, of course," David answered, giving Zach his pat answer for delaying a commitment to an unexpected request. "There are a lot of things to consider."

"I'd like to contact a friend of mine in Denver to get him to fly you here in his private plane so we can talk. Can you get away this weekend?"

"I'm not sure." The opportunity to make a quick trip to Montana and check on Melissa and the boys was more on his mind than discussing Zachary's proposition. "Why don't I give you a call this eve-ning, when I've had a chance to mull this over?"

"Good enough." Zachary spent a moment on pleasantries and then signed off with "Talk to you later."

After the judge hung up, David leaned back in his

chair and laughed so loudly that Elsie poked her head in his office.

"Are you all right?" She frowned, obviously puzzled by his outburst.

"What would you say if I told you I just might decide to join a law firm in the fair state of Montana?"

"I'd say you've lost your mind. You're not serious?"

He shook his head, still chuckling. "No, of course not. I just think it's a joke on me that after all the work and effort I've put into a Colorado political career, someone wants me to leave it all behind, and move to Montana."

On Saturday afternoon, when Melissa opened the door and saw David standing there, she stared at him as if he were some kind of apparition.

"Just thought I'd drop by and say hello." His grin was disarming. "Surprised?"

"Amazed. What are you doing here?"

"I'm trying to figure that out myself. May I come in?"

She stepped back as he came into the house, her thoughts whirling like dry leaves whipped by the wind. For days, she'd been trying to figure out how she and the boys could get back to Denver without calling him. And now, here he was.

"I've missed you." He searched her face. "Aren't you glad to see me?"

As he reached for her, all her defenses against involving him in her life again were leveled. Her voice was threaded with a sudden emotion that threatened to well up and choke her. She whispered, "Yes, I missed you."

When he kissed her, the warmth of his lips brought back a storm of memories of the tender and tense moments they'd shared on the trip. He let one hand trace the curve of her cheek, and then he rested the side of his face against hers. For a moment, they just stood there without moving, until Scruffy appeared at the top of the stairs.

Recognizing David, he came bounding down the stairs, leaping into the air, woofing and wagging his tail, as if trying to get airborne. Both David and Melissa laughed at the dog's exuberant attack on him.

"Whoa! Whoa!" David picked up Scruffy and was treated to a barrage of wet, licking kisses. "Easy, fellow, easy."

The boys appeared at the top of the stairs, wondering what the commotion was all about. They squealed and bounded down, calling his name.

"Slow down," Melissa ordered, laughing, afraid they'd land flat on their faces before they reached the bottom.

"How ya doing, cowpokes?" David asked, giving them a hug. "I see you're still wearing your boots."

They both started talking at once, and Richie grabbed his hand to show him their room. Eric grabbed David's other hand, and the two boys pulled him toward the stairs.

"I guess I don't have a choice," he said, smiling at Melissa over their heads. "Don't go away. We need to talk."

"Yes, we do," she said as steadily as she could, considering that her pulse was racing wildly from the unexpected warmth of his embrace and kiss.

As she watched the three of them climb the stairs and disappear into the hallway, her emotions were suddenly under siege. Was she strong enough to stay the course of her convictions and turn away from a love that promised nothing but conflict for both of them? He had pulled her into his arms before she'd had a chance to think. It scared her to realize how much she loved him.

She walked slowly through the house and out to the patio, where Paula was sunning herself.

Paula opened her eyes and asked, "Was someone at the door? I heard Scruffy making a ruckus."

"A real surprise. David's here. He's upstairs with the boys, looking over their posters."

"How wonderful. I've been wanting to meet him and thank him personally for all he did for me. Everyone's been telling me what a terrific guy he is, and I've noticed a special sparkle in your eyes when his name is mentioned." Her smile faded as she noticed Melissa's face. "What's the matter? From your expression, I'd guess you're not feeling very happy about his visit."

"I don't know how I feel." She plopped down in a chair and took a couple of deep breaths. "When he's around, it's hard to keep my head on straight. Why does life have to be so complicated?"

"I don't know, but it just seems to be human nature to make it that way." Paula smiled. "Why don't you just relax and see what happens? Somebody said that worrying is the wrong kind of praying.''

Melissa chuckled. ''That sounds like something my grandmother would have said.''

When David joined them, Eric and Richie were hanging onto him as if they were determined not to let him get away again. The way he was laughing and joking with them made Melissa wonder if he had any idea what he was doing to them. Didn't he realize that he was just setting them up for more disappointment and rejection?

Paula asked David polite questions about his work and how long he planned to stay in Wolfton.

''Until Monday. I have the weekend.''

''Good, you can go to church with us tomorrow. Skip and Carol will be delighted, and so will all the other folks who would like to meet you.''

David didn't know how to politely refuse Paula without causing hard feelings. He just wanted to spend Sunday persuading Melissa that it was time for her and the boys to return to Denver. Zachary had scheduled a meeting with him on Monday, even though David had warned him that he didn't feel that leaving Colorado was in his best interest.

Paula got to her feet. ''Why don't I take the boys inside for milk and cookies, and let you two have some privacy? You'll stay for dinner, of course. I believe Zach is bringing some fresh trout. He's quite a fisherman. Nobody can reel in a fighting fish the way he can,'' she said proudly.

As soon as Paula had disappeared into the kitchen

with the boys, Melissa turned to David. "She and Zachary are getting married."

He started to tell her that he already knew, but changed his mind. "How soon?"

"I don't know, but the boys and I can't stay here as I had hoped. And I don't see any alternative other than to go back to Denver."

He nodded, relieved. Good, that was settled. He was afraid that she'd come up with another plan for her and boys to stay in Wolfton. Once he got her back to Denver, he'd have a chance to change her mind about a lot of things.

"I don't understand how you got here," she said, puzzled, suddenly realizing she hadn't seen any car parked in front of the house.

He told her then about the private plane that had brought him. "I took a taxi from the airstrip. Can you and the boys be ready to fly back with me on Monday afternoon?"

Melissa shook her head. "No, I've promised to help Paula with wedding preparations. And she wants the boys, as part of her family, to be here."

"How long will that be?"

"They haven't set a date yet, but I'm sure it will be soon. Now that Paula's made up her mind, she won't want to wait."

David wasn't happy about the delay, but there was little he could do about it. He'd have to fly back on Monday without her. He hoped that she would never know about the opportunity that Zachary Daniels was offering him. She'd never understand why he couldn't spend his life in a small pond when he had been raised to swim with big fish in the political world. He intended to thank Zachary for his offer of a law partnership, and be on his way.

He was grateful that the subject wasn't mentioned at dinner. Apparently Zachary hadn't said anything to Paula, and the conversation remained general. David had little time for any private conversation with Melissa that evening, but he was glad that he would have all day Sunday to be with her. He decided that Zachary and Paula had done him a big favor by deciding to get married. Melissa ought to know by now that there wasn't any future for her or the boys in Wolfton.

Chapter Sixteen

"Wonderful to see you again," Carol greeted David at the front door of the church. "It's perfect that you should be here today of all days."

David shot a look at Melissa. Was this some kind of special day that he should know about? Her expression was as blank as his.

As they walked toward the front door, Carol scooted the boys on ahead. "I'll bet your Sunday School teacher is waiting for you. You know where to go, don't you?"

Both Eric and Richie nodded and bounded up the front steps, racing to see who'd be first. "Slow down," Melissa ordered in a motherly fashion. She hoped they didn't burst into their classroom like a couple of wild animals.

Carol turned to Melissa and David. "Let's go into Skip's study. I have some great news for you."

"What kind of news?" Melissa prodded as they followed Carol into a room lined with bookshelves and furnished with an old-fashioned desk and comfortable armchairs.

"Have a seat." Carol waved to the chairs but remained standing, hugging herself as if she couldn't bear to sit quietly for even a minute.

"What is it, Carol?" Melissa couldn't imagine what kind of news had put that twinkle in her bright eyes. "You look ready to burst."

"I have a wonderful surprise. Truly. Truly."

"And we would love to hear it," David said with a smile.

"All right." She took a deep breath. "Are you ready for this? Jim and Nancy Becker have generously agreed to adopt Eric and Richie. They know what it would mean to Paula to keep the boys here, and they're willing to take them."

The ticking of an old-fashioned clock was the only sound in the pastor's study for several seconds. Melissa looked at Carol, uncertain whether she had heard correctly.

"Jim Becker?" David repeated, frowning.

"Are you sure?" Melissa prodded.

"Yes, I'm sure. What's the matter with you two?" Carol looked puzzled. "Don't you understand? I give you the answer you've been looking for, and you act like a couple of sleepwalkers." She looked from one to the other in amazement.

"I'm just stunned, that's all," Melissa said quickly.

"You've been looking for a loving Christian home for the boys, and you won't find any better than Nancy and Jim's," Carol insisted.

"When did all this happen?" David asked, as if he

was going to need a lot more information about these two people before giving his approval.

"Jim and Nancy came over to the house last night and told us what they were thinking," Carol said. "A few days ago I shared with Nancy the fact that you'd brought Eric and Richie to visit Paula with the hope that she would be able to keep them. Since Jim really feels close to Paula and Nancy loves children, they decided that raising her great-nephews instead of turning them over to strangers was the right thing to do."

"And they're financially able to assume the added expense of raising them?" David asked bluntly.

"Of course. Jim has a secure job with the fire department," Carol assured him.

David searched Melissa's face. "You like Jim and Nancy, don't you?"

"I really don't know them all that well," she answered hesitantly. "Jim seems like a nice fellow, and Nancy is very sweet. I guess they're old enough to handle the demands of two active boys," she said as if trying to convince herself.

"I've only talked to Jim a couple of times, and our conversation was nothing personal," David said.

"Trust me. You won't find a better home for the boys," Carol said, obviously surprised that her good news had met with such reservations.

"We probably need a little time to think about this," Melissa said, forcing a smile.

"Yes, of course." Carol looked at both of them as if she didn't have a clue as to what was going on. "You'll join us for Sunday dinner, won't you. We can talk more then. It's a little late for Sunday School.

Why don't you stay here until it's time for church service?''

Melissa nodded, and Carol slipped out of the study and closed the door behind her.

David searched Melissa's face and hated the empty look in her eyes. When he reached over and took her hand, it was cold to the touch. "What is it?"

"I'm not sure," she admitted. "Maybe I'm just stunned. I don't know why I have reservations about this. Could be that I'm letting my personal feelings cloud my judgment. Come on, let's go sit in the sanctuary. It'll be empty for another half-hour while everyone is in the classrooms." She needed to let her thoughts settle in prayerful silence, and ask for some divine guidance.

A few minutes later, as they sat together in the sanctuary, Melissa bent her head in quiet contemplation, and David tried to think about the situation in a detached, rational manner. For some reason he was as negative about the Beckers taking the boys as Melissa was. Maybe he felt that the young couple were just doing it out of their affection for Paula, and not because they were really taken with Eric and Richie.

As the church began filling up with Sunday worshipers, David was surprised how many people nodded and smiled at him. He recognized some of the men who had been in the search party, and several of the women who had brought food for the celebration at Paula's house. They seemed genuinely happy to see him, and he enjoyed the comfortable feeling of belonging that comes to people who have shared a traumatic experience.

When the organ music began, Skip appeared, solemnly dressed in his clerical robe. He smiled broadly at David. A few minutes later, when the children filed in and sat in the front pews for a short Bible story, Eric and Richie kept twisting around and waving at Melissa and David.

Their eyes were bright and their mouths spread in wide grins as they filed out with the others to go downstairs for the children's service.

As David sat in the radius of sunlight pouring through multi-stained windows, he sensed a oneness with those around him. He experienced a sense of wholeness and completeness that he'd never felt before. At first he didn't know how to handle it, this knowledge that he was not alone or separated as he had believed all his life. He didn't know how it had happened, but he realized that is wasn't power and prestige that were important in life. Melissa's God of Love had reached out to him, and as the swell of organ music poured over him, he gave Melissa a knowing smile and saw her eyes suddenly mist with tears.

The Reverend Skip Carlson based his sermon on Mark 8:36. "For what does it profit a man to gain the whole world and forfeit his life?"

In a nonjudgmental way, Skip challenged his congregation to consider the choices in their lives, and to look to the Lord for the courage to change that which was keeping them from the abundant lives that the Bible promised.

Melissa tried to guess what David might be thinking. Was he even listening, or was he just worried

about the time he was wasting spending this Sunday
morning in church? His expression didn't reveal anything about his reaction to the service or Skip's sermon.

After the closing hymn, they joined other worshipers moving toward the open doors, and were stopped
repeatedly by people who introduced themselves and
shook David's hand. When Melissa deserted him to
get the boys, he was left to handle all the attention as
best he could.

Finally, at the door, Skip shook hands with him and
smiled broadly. "Great to have you with us this
morning, David."

"You really hit me between the eyes with some of
the things you had to say," David admitted. "I took
a good look at my life in a way I never have before,
and a couple of lightbulbs went on."

"We call them 'God moments,'" Skip said. "It's
amazing how suddenly things make more sense if you
see them with God's truth."

"I haven't had any practice looking at life that
way," David confessed. "But I know that something
is missing."

"All the Lord needs is a willing heart," Skip assured him. "And the courage of a man to follow
him."

At that moment Zachary joined them, smiling
broadly. "Well, now, I'd say you're a pretty popular
fellow around here, David. Just the kind of partner
that could make our firm the best in the state. After
our meeting tomorrow, I hope you'll have a positive
answer for me."

"You don't have to wait until tomorrow, Zachary. I can give you my decision now." He took a deep breath. "If things go the way I hope with Melissa, yes, I would like very much to accept your offer of partnership."

"I knew you were one smart fellow." Zachary grinned.

Skip put his hand on David's shoulder. "Wonderful! It's amazing how things fall into place when the good Lord gets involved."

"I'm going to be needing some heavenly help when I talk with Melissa."

"You'll have it," Skip promised.

Melissa was openly puzzled when David arranged for the boys to go home with the Carlsons, and suggested that they leave the Jeep in the church parking lot and walk the few blocks to Skip and Carol's house. But she was relieved to have the extra time to get her thoughts in order. Her prayers for understanding had not brought the kind of peace she needed.

"I have something to tell you." David took her hand as they walked slowly along the tree-shaded street.

She could see that he was struggling to find the right words, and this hesitant manner was not like him. "What is it?"

"I had a call from Zachary last week. He's retiring from the bench and asked me if I'd be interested in a full partnership in his law firm."

"Here in Wolfton?" Her eyes widened. "Why would he think you'd even consider it?"

"If you want to know the truth, I came here with every intention of turning it down, but I've decided to accept his offer."

She stared at him as if the whole thing was too preposterous to be taken seriously. "Is this some kind of bad joke?"

"It's no joke. I'm serious."

"You can't mean it." She shook her head in disbelief. "Why would you give up everything—?"

"That's the point exactly," he interrupted. "I don't want to give up everything. I almost realized too late that everything that really matters to me is here." He stopped in the middle of the sidewalk and gently turned her around to face him. "Skip's message this morning was like a strong lens that put everything in my life into focus. Now, I know what has been missing, and I'm ready to accept a whole different view of spiritual values. I know I can't rearrange all my thinking and beliefs overnight, but I'm ready to try. I don't want to give up you and the boys. Not now, not ever."

"What about your political ambitions?"

"I want to quit marching to the world's drummer and find a deeper meaning for my life. I've been slow to realize that it's my love for you and the boys that is really important. Skip told me that all the Lord wants is for me to follow my heart—and that leads me straight to you."

She was suddenly so full of happiness that she had trouble breathing. She had prayed for a moment like this, but listening to him say the words that she'd been longing to hear was truly a miracle.

"I'll do my best to be the kind of husband and father that will make you happy. I'm asking you again, Melissa, and this time, please, say yes. Will you marry me?"

Without hesitation, she lifted her face to his. "Yes, I will."

He kissed her tenderly as they sealed their commitment in the middle of the sidewalk on a lovely Sunday afternoon. When someone in a car honked, they looked up and saw Paula grinning at them, as she and Zach drove by.

Laughing, David put his arm around Melissa's waist and they walked happily together, just smiling and feeling in harmony.

About a block away from the Carlson's house, a moving van was pulling away from a beautifully restored Victorian house, and they saw a couple with three children loading belongings into a van parked in the driveway.

Melissa slowed her steps as she gazed at the Queen Anne-style house that was nestled in a frame of tall trees. She was startled by how much the white house reminded her of a picture that her grandmother had always had on her bedroom wall. A wide, old-fashioned veranda circled the ground floor of the two-story house, intricate lacy bargeboards had been freshly painted white, and several brick chimneys rose from the mansard roof. There was even a round turret room with picturesque dormer windows.

David could tell from the rapt expression on her face that she was taken with the house. "Want to take a look inside?"

"Do you think we should?"

"Why not? There's a Realtor's sign on the lawn."

"But we're not potential buyers."

"Who says we're not? We're going to need a house to live in, aren't we? You just agreed to marry me, remember?"

"Yes, but this house is way too big and expensive."

He just laughed and guided her down the sidewalk. When they asked the young couple moving out of the house if they could look around, the woman looked a little hesitant. "It's really in a mess. I mean, the cleaning people are coming tomorrow. I think the Realtor is going to have an open house in a few days."

Her husband only laughed. "It's all right, honey. They're not here to see how clean we're leaving the place." He motioned them into the house. "Take a look. If you like it, you can come back for a second look."

Arm-in-arm they walked through the rooms. The first floor had a large entry hall, a large parlor with a bay window and marble fireplace, a sitting room, dining room, kitchen, pantry, maid's room, closets and a bathroom. A handsome oak staircase let to the second floor, and four bedrooms, two bathrooms and a sitting room.

Melissa seemed to love everything about the house, and her appreciation of its historical heritage was evident to David in the way she pointed out all the intricate woodwork, embossed ceilings and vintage details.

David just smiled and nodded, enjoying her enthusiasm. When they'd completed their tour of the entire house, he asked, "Well, what do you think? Should we buy it?"

"You mean…to live in?"

"Isn't that what people do with a house they buy?" he teased.

The wonder she felt that this beautiful old house might actually become the home she had always dreamed about was almost too much to handle. "Do you really mean it?"

He just laughed and kissed the tip of her nose. "Yes, I really mean it."

The man greeted them hopefully at the front door. "Well, what do you think? It's a great house for a family. Do you have children?"

"Yes, we have two sons," David said readily. "Two wonderful little boys. Their names are Eric and Richie."

At that moment, Melissa knew what it was like to experience happiness "pressed down, shaken together and overflowing."

* * * * *

Dear Reader,

I am delighted to share with you the tender story of Melissa and David as they experience the truth of God's promise, "I will lead you in the path that you should go." Melissa and David had their own ideas about handling the situation facing them, and the lesson of "letting go, and letting God" was not an easy one for either of them to learn.

Melissa's faith and confidence wavered when her plans didn't work out. Thwarted at every turn, she found her impatience put her at odds with God's divine timing. Only when all her efforts failed and she released the outcome to God was He able to open the windows of heaven and pour out an unexpected blessing upon her.

Although David was a generous person at heart, his political ambitions blinded him to the real treasures in life. He allowed the world's pressures, his parents' expectations and his own willfulness to control his life. Only when the love in his heart became more important than his ego was he able to turn his life in the direction that God had planned for him, and realize the true meaning of spiritual happiness.

I enjoy hearing from readers of my books. You can reach me c/o Steeple Hill Books, 300 E. 42nd Street, New York, NY 10017.

Leona Karr

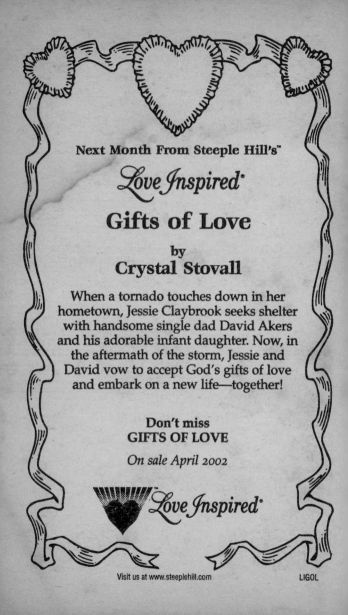

Next Month From Steeple Hill's™

Love Inspired®

Gifts of Love

by
Crystal Stovall

When a tornado touches down in her
hometown, Jessie Claybrook seeks shelter
with handsome single dad David Akers
and his adorable infant daughter. Now, in
the aftermath of the storm, Jessie and
David vow to accept God's gifts of love
and embark on a new life—together!

**Don't miss
GIFTS OF LOVE**

On sale April 2002

Love Inspired®

**Next Month From
Steeple Hill's™**

Love Inspired®

Something Beautiful

by
Lenora Worth

Daredevil Lucas Dorsette relishes flirting
with danger. However, the reckless pilot
discovers a new appreciation for life
when he falls in love with a stunning
supermodel who shows him the true
meaning of courage. But will their faith
help them face an uncertain future?

**Don't miss
SOMETHING BEAUTIFUL**

On sale April 2002

Love Inspired®